# The Portrait

By

Dawn Woods

Grosvenor House
Publishing Limited

All rights reserved
Copyright © Dawn Woods, 2024

The right of Dawn Woods to be identified as the author of this
work has been asserted in accordance with Section 78
of the Copyright, Designs and Patents Act 1988

The book cover is copyright to Dawn Woods

This book is published by
Grosvenor House Publishing Ltd
Link House
140 The Broadway, Tolworth, Surrey, KT6 7HT.
www.grosvenorhousepublishing.co.uk

This book is sold subject to the conditions that it shall not, by way of
trade or otherwise, be lent, resold, hired out or otherwise circulated
without the author's or publisher's prior consent in any form of
binding or cover other than that in which it is published and
without a similar condition including this condition being
imposed on the subsequent purchaser.

This book is a work of fiction. Any resemblance to
people or events, past or present, is purely coincidental.

A CIP record for this book
is available from the British Library

ISBN 978-1-80381-745-3
eBook ISBN 978-1-80381-815-3

With thanks to my dear friend
Alan for his help and support

And in remembrance of
my much-missed Mum and Dad

# Acknowledgements

With much gratitude to Grosvenor House Publishing Limited, especially to Jasmine who helped me greatly during the process of publishing my book.

Thanks also go to Knutsford IT and The Flock of Arts Knutsford.

# One

He had found it at last, tucked away in the churchyard where all the old graves from past centuries lay, some almost worn away. But luckily for Richard, the one he had been looking for was intact, and readable. Even the rose, although worn, was still visible above the inscription:

Catherine Anne Courtney
26 June 1805–28 SEPTEMBER 1828

There were more words written below, but time and the weather had worn them away and, together with the lichen, made them unreadable.

It was now August 1928, so the stone was almost 100 years old.

Richard stared at it, then looked around. It was a warm, sunny, but breezy day. The wind rustled the leaves on the trees and the long grasses which had grown between the stones. There was a pretty stone church nearby. It was quiet and peaceful, and he wondered if it would have been better to have stayed in a hotel in the small town nearby, rather than Bordeaux, which was busy and quite noisy.

He was a handsome man in his mid-30s, with dark brown hair and a moustache. He always dressed well. Even today, in the heat, he was wearing cream slacks and a light blue shirt open at the collar, with a cream summer jacket over it. He had come to France from his home in England, to research a book he hoped to write on the history of the manor where he now lived. He had almost finished his research work, and carried an attaché case that contained most of his findings. He was a little disappointed there were a few gaps in the information he had gathered on Catherine, but thought he would have enough to be able to begin his book on his return home.

He suddenly felt thirsty (it had been a long morning), and he decided to drive to the nearby town and have a drink. He found a small café, but when he went inside it was almost full. There was one table left. He took off his jacket, and whilst he turned to put it on the coat stand, a young lady walked in carrying a handbag. She was passing Richard just as he turned around, and he bumped into her, knocking her bag to the floor. He stooped to pick it up, and handed it back to her. "Pardon, mademoiselle," he said.

The young woman smiled as she took the bag from him. "That's all right, thank you," she said, smiling.

Richard was a little surprised she spoke English. "Not a lot of room, I'm afraid," he said. "But please, you have this table, I'll find somewhere else."

"That's very kind, but I couldn't, really. You were here first." She turned to leave.

"Then perhaps we could share?" he said.

She looked a little uncertain. "Well, I don't think—"

"Please," he said smiling. "I'd enjoy the company."

She was still not sure, but said, "Well, if you don't mind." Richard pulled a seat out for her and she sat down. "Thank you," she said a little shyly.

Richard sat down and handed her a menu.

She raised her hand. "Thank you, no. I'm just having a drink".

"Me too," he said, replacing the menu.

A waitress came over, pencil and pad in hand. He looked across the table. "What would you like?" he asked.

"Oh no, it's all right thank you, I'll get my own".

"Nonsense," replied Richard. "I'd like to buy you a drink – as my guest."

She was about to object again, but thought better of it. "Then I shall have a coffee, please."

"*Deux café, S'il vous plaît.*" The waitress nodded and walked away.

"You speak French?" said the young woman, smiling.

"Not as well as your English, I'm afraid. Just bits and pieces to get me by." Feeling the awkwardness between them, he took out a cigarette case and offered her a cigarette.

"No, thank you, I don't smoke."

"Oh. Then do you mind if—"

"No, please do." Her accent was soft, and her face small and beautiful, framed with shoulder-length, dark brown hair. Richard thought she was probably in her mid-20s. As he lit the cigarette, conversation began, a little awkwardly at first.

"Nice weather we've been having," said Richard.

"Yes, it is now, but was rather wet last month." She looked at his handsome features, a little tanned by recent weather. "You're here on holiday?" she asked.

"Well, I suppose you could call it a working holiday. I've been doing research for a book I'm hoping to write."

"Oh, you're a writer? How interesting."

"Well, actually I have a publishing business that I took over when my parents died, but yes, I do write from time to time."

The waitress brought the coffee. "Mademoiselle, monsieur." They both thanked her, and she moved away.

"What is it about, this book?" asked the young woman, taking a sip of her coffee.

"It's a historical piece on my home, or rather I should say, about the chap who lived there in the early 19th century. But it is his wife who has brought me to France. She's buried in the cemetery, just outside the town."

"Oh, I see," she said. "But how did this English lady come to be buried in France?"

Richard took a pull on his cigarette. "She was a French girl. She married an English man, Thomas Courtney. He was, up until the time of his death, squire of the estate, and lived in the manor where I now live."

She was clearly impressed. "It sounds very grand."

Richard smiled proudly. "Well yes, I must admit it's a beautiful place."

"A country seat handed down from generation to generation?" she asked.

"Actually, no. In fact, it had been empty for many years, and was almost beyond repair. After the death of my parents, I had the resources available to bring it back to its former glory."

"I see," she replied.

He took a pull on his cigarette and knocked the ash into the ashtray. "I've almost finished my research on Thomas's wife, Catherine, so I could go home earlier than I thought."

THE PORTRAIT

"That's a great pity," she said, and took a sip of coffee. Then, suddenly embarrassed, "I mean, the weather is so lovely now it would be a shame to miss it."

There was a long silence; one of those moments when somebody would say there must be an angel passing overhead. Suddenly Richard said, "May I say, you speak remarkably good English. Does it help with your work?"

"Not really," she replied. "I work in a dress shop in the town, although we do get tourists from time to time. Some of them are English, so it gives me an opportunity to practice. I learned English as a girl, just as an interest, but seemed to pick it up quite well."

"Do your parents live locally?" he asked.

"My parents were killed in a train crash when I was two. My aunt brought me up. She lived in Bordeaux. When she died I came to live and work here."

"I see," he said quietly. "I'm so sorry, I didn't mean to pry."

"That's all right," she said, picking up her handbag. "But I really must be going." She stood up to leave. "Thank you for letting me share your table." She fumbled in her bag for her purse.

"No," said Richard, standing up. "Please, let me."

She smiled. "Oh no. Really, I couldn't."

"Nonsense," he replied. "I asked you to sit here as my guest."

"Well, all right then. You're very kind. Thank you very much." She turned to leave. As she walked away, she looked back at him. "Oh, and I wish you luck with your book."

"Thank you," he said as he watched her walk out of the door. Quickly, he paid the waitress, picked up his attaché case, grabbed his jacket and rushed after her. "Mademoiselle, excuse me." She turned towards him as he approached her. "I'm sorry to shout out in the street like that, and please don't think I make a habit of picking up strange women, but—"

She stifled a smile. "I'm a strange woman?"

Richard looked embarrassed. "Oh no, of course not." He gave a short, nervous laugh. "Whatever must you think of me? And I don't think the words 'picking up' are quite right, either." He abstractly smoothed his hair back with his hand. "Oh Lord, I'm making a real mess of this," he smiled. "It's just that, well, it's been a long, tiring morning and I thought—" He paused a moment, then resolutely said, "Well, the fact is, I'd deem it an honour if you would have dinner with me tonight."

She was a little uncertain. "Well…"

Richard was embarrassed. "Oh, it's all right. You're probably busy or have other arrangements." Then he suddenly realised. "Oh, I never thought: you're married, aren't you?"

"No, I'm not married." She smiled, as she softened towards him. "And yes I would love to have dinner with you."

Richard looked relieved. "Really? Oh, that's splendid. I'll look forward to it." He suddenly realised they didn't know each other's names. "I suppose we'd better introduce ourselves. My name is Richard Anderson, but please call me Richard." He offered her his hand.

She took it and said, "And my name is Miss Moreau, but you must call me Yvette."

# Two

That evening they entered a beautiful restaurant in Bordeaux. It was filled with diners dripping opulence. The lighting was subdued, and there was a pianist playing Chopin's finest pieces. The waiter approached them with two menus, which he handed to them as soon as they were seated.

It was a memorable evening, one which Richard thought he would never forget. Yvette wore a beautiful light blue evening dress, her hair fashioned into a French plait, and a necklace with a pale blue stone around her slender neck. She was more beautiful than he thought, and indeed they made a handsome couple as they sat there, each enjoying their evening, and each other's company. Later that night, Richard's car drew up outside a small terraced house in the dimly lit street on which Yvette lived. Richard got out of the car and walked round to open the car door for her. As he walked her to the door, she smiled at him.

"Thank you so much for a wonderful evening."

"On the contrary, it's I who should be thanking you. I don't know when I've enjoyed myself more." He looked at her a moment, then said, "Would you find it presumptuous of me if I were to ask you out again? A picnic perhaps? That is, if the weather holds out."

"I would look forward to it very much," she replied.

Richard was pleased. "Oh, well in that case how would Sunday suit you?"

"Sunday would suit me very well," she smiled.

"Right, well Sunday it is then." He looked at her a moment then took her hand and kissed it. "Thank you again for tonight," he said.

Yvette was touched by his courteous manner, and as he let go of her hand she said, "Until Sunday, then."

Richard walked back to the car as Yvette looked after him. Before he got in he said, "I'll pick you up about 2pm, if that's all right?"

"Yes, thank you," she smiled. "2pm will be fine."

That Sunday turned out to be a beautiful day, in more ways than one.

Richard and Yvette were sitting by the lakeside. Yvette was watching the birds on the water; Richard was having difficulty opening a bottle of wine. "Nearly there," he said.

Yvette picked up two glasses in anticipation of the cork popping. When it did, it was as if it had taken them by surprise, and they started laughing as Richard began to pour. Later, after they'd eaten, they sat watching the birds on the water. Richard smiled at Yvette but she was staring pensively across the lake. Richard watched her, wondering what she was thinking about. Then she suddenly became aware he was looking at her. She smiled, and he kissed her.

After that, they saw each other every day. There were trips to the theatre, dining out, and walking arm in arm through the park. One day, they could be seen walking along a street in Bordeaux. They were looking in the window of a jeweller's shop.

That night, they dined out at the same restaurant they'd gone to on their first date together. Their table was candlelit, and the pianist was playing a selection of romantic music. Richard took out the engagement ring and slipped it onto Yvette's finger. They smiled at each other across the table, then toasted each other with champagne.

# Three

**Shearwater Manor, Berkshire, England**

The season was changing as August ended and September began. But it was a bright sunny afternoon when they arrived at the manor. The house was just visible as they entered through the wrought iron gates on to the long tree-lined driveway. It was bordered by immaculate lawns, with parkland beyond; older, larger trees here and there, their leaves just turning ever so lightly to copper. The manor was 17th century, still in its original style, and had been sympathetically renovated, the mullioned windows glinting in the sunshine. Yvette was stunned by what she saw.

"Richard, it's beautiful."

Richard smiled, pleased. "Yes," he said. "I sometimes can't believe it's my home. And yours too now, darling." He took hold of her hand and kissed it.

As they drew nearer, Yvette's expression changed. She looked thoughtful for a moment, then dismissed it and smiled again. The car continued on to what was once a carriage sweep at the front of the house. Five steps led to the main door, with two carriage lamps either side. As Richard got out of the car, the butler, Maurice, came down the steps with a younger manservant: Johnathan. He opened the car door for Yvette. She thanked him as she stepped out, then he went to remove the luggage from the car. Richard was already standing with Maurice who welcomed them both, then went to help Johnathan. Yvette stood looking over the lawns, with Richard standing beside her.

"It's stunning, isn't it?" he said, proudly.

Yvette didn't reply. She looked thoughtful again.

Then Richard took her arm. "Come on," he said. "We'll have some tea."

They walked up the steps and into the house, but from the lawns, someone was watching…

The hallway was large with a staircase running up the middle, and branching both left and right at the top. There were several doors off the hallway, leading to various rooms, one of which led to the kitchens, utility rooms and servants' quarters at the back of the house. The paintings and décor had been tastefully done to be in keeping with their surroundings, and a large window at the top of the staircase streamed light into the hallway below.

As Richard took off his coat, Maurice appeared. "May I say it is good to have you home. I trust your trip was an enjoyable one?"

"Yes, Maurice, thank you. I think I should introduce you to my fiancée, Miss Moreau."

Yvette had been looking around the hallway thoughtfully. Richard interrupted her thoughts.

"Darling!"

Yvette was suddenly aware. "Oh, I'm so sorry."

"This is Maurice," continued Richard. "He's been with me since I came here. Three years, isn't it, Maurice?"

"Yes indeed, sir." He smiled at Yvette. "How do you do, miss? I trust you are well?"

"Yes, very well, thank you," she replied.

"May I take your coat, miss?"

"Thank you, Maurice," she said, as he helped her off with her coat. She put the gloves she was holding into her handbag.

"Would you care to see your room, miss?"

Richard looked at Yvette. She looked tired. "I think we'd like some tea first, Maurice," he said. "It's been a long drive."

"Certainly, sir. I'll bring it to the sitting room. We lit the fire in there earlier, it felt rather chilly."

"Thank you, Maurice."

Yvette shivered and rubbed her arm.

"You're cold," Richard said.

Yvette smiled weakly. "Just a little."

He took her arm. "Come on, we'll soon have you warm." Richard led her to the sitting room, closed the door behind them, and walked towards the French windows, on the left of which stood a drinks cabinet with various decanters and glasses. He looked briefly over the garden. There were shrubs either side of the lawn, in the middle of which was a stone cherub. Rose bushes adorned the borders. The parkland beyond was fenced off, with its mature trees dotted here and there in the distance. Richard turned and picked up the decanters one by one. He chose the brandy and poured out two drinks. He walked over to Yvette, who was still standing by the door. "Here you are, darling. Come and sit down and have a brandy. It'll warm you up until the tea arrives."

Yvette absently took the glass from him, but continued to look around the room. It was very spacious, with various furniture of the period. Two armchairs were set either side of the roaring log fire, with a settee placed in front of it. There was an elaborate clock on the mantel which chimed the hour, and Yvette turned to face it. Then her gaze travelled above the mantel where hanged the portrait of a man, probably in his late 20s, with dark hair and a handsome face. He was dressed smartly in the clothes of the 19th century. Painted behind him was the view from the sitting room window. It was not quite the view as it was now. The garden itself was quite similar, with a profusion of shrubs and roses, and a stone cherub in the centre, not that different from the one which stood there today. The parkland stretched beyond, but the fencing was different, and the trees were a lot smaller than they were now. She looked at the figure of the man. He was standing beside an empty chair, with his hand resting on the back of it, and he was smiling.

Richard had already sat down on the settee, and he patted the cushion beside him. "Come on, darling, sit down."

Yvette sat down and took a sip of her brandy, but her gaze travelled once again to the portrait.

"You weren't cold in the car, were you, darling?" asked Richard.

"No. It was only in the hallway, when I took my coat off, I suppose. I'm all right now." She smiled at him but then looked once more at the portrait.

"Handsome fellow, wouldn't you say?" said Richard.

"Who is he?" she asked.

"May I introduce you to Thomas Courtney, squire of this estate 100 years ago?"

Yvette was thoughtful. "Thomas Courtney... That name seems familiar."

"Yes, I mentioned him the very first time we met. Remember, the café? It is thanks to him or rather his wife that we met." He took a drink.

"Yes, I remember. His wife was French." She put her glass down on a small table by the settee. "Was the portrait hanging there when you bought the house?"

"Good Lord, no. It was found in one of the rooms upstairs. I had it restored. It was in a dreadful mess; I almost threw it out. I'm glad now I didn't." He finished his drink and put the glass down. He leaned back and put his arm on the back of the settee behind her. Yvette leaned back and rested against him, then he moved his arm down onto her shoulders. "Finding it was the reason I wanted to research the history of the man. And I suppose, inadvertently, how I came to meet you." He turned Yvette's face towards him, and they kissed. Just then Maurice came in with the tea trolley, on which stood a silver teapot, another pot with hot water, sugar bowl, milk and a selection of sandwiches and cakes. Yvette pulled away from Richard, embarrassed.

"Excuse me, sir, miss."

Richard looked at the trolley. "You've excelled yourself, Maurice."

"Mrs Worth thought you and Miss Moreau may be hungry after your long drive. I hope everything is in order?"

"Very nice, Maurice, thank you. And thank Mrs Worth for me."

"I will, sir. Would you like me to pour?"

"No, that's all right, Maurice, we'll manage, thank you."

"Very good, sir." And with that he left the room.

"That was embarrassing," smiled Yvette.

"Oh, don't mind Maurice, he's a good sort. You'll have to get used to him being around. He's the only one who lives in. We have a cleaning lady, Mrs Parker, and her daughter Sarah, who come in each day; Mrs Worth, the cook, and Benson the groom and his stable lad Joe, who looks after the horses, does the gardening and odd jobs."

"Oh yes, your horses. How many did you tell me you had?"

"Three. I'll show them to you tomorrow. I know you've never ridden, but it's so pleasant, especially with the countryside around here."

"I rode on a pony once, when my aunt and I were on holiday. I was only about six years old," she smiled.

"It would be a nice hobby for you. I can teach you."

Yvette felt a little uncertain, but she said nothing. She took hold of the teapot. "Shall I pour?"

"If you wish," replied Richard.

As she poured she asked, "Will you be starting your book soon?"

"Probably," he said, as he took a sandwich. "But for now, I have better ways to fill my time." He smiled at Yvette.

"Why is there a vacant chair in the portrait? Do you know?" she asked as she handed Richard his tea.

"That's what I wondered. Apparently, according to some records found after his death, the chair was for Catherine. It was so tragic, the way it all ended."

"But how did it end? You never told me much about it," said Yvette.

"I thought we had better things to talk about," smiled Richard. "And I didn't want to bore you."

"It wouldn't bore me. I'm interested," she answered.

Richard considered her a moment as he finished his sandwich. Then resignedly, although pleased at her interest, he took a sip of tea, then got up and walked over to the fire, putting down his cup and saucer on a small table by the fireplace. He took a cigarette case from his pocket and, standing with his back to the fire, lit a cigarette. He took a pull on it, and blew the smoke out slowly, then he began to speak. "Well, all his troubles began way back in the 19th century, 1824 to be exact, when he was a young man of 24. He lived here virtually alone, apart from the servants and his mother, Elizabeth, his father having died two years earlier, leaving Thomas, as the only heir, the responsibility and status of owning Shearwater.

"He was a well-educated man, and treated his tenants and staff fairly, which made him well liked. However, there was no more socialising at the manor. His mother preferred, instead, to keep the manor very much to herself and her son." Richard took another pull at his cigarette. "It was because of this Thomas took to riding out to the village inn occasionally, to try his luck at the gaming tables, with a good friend of his called Charles Brent. Apparently, Thomas and Charles had grown up together and were like brothers. It was on one of these nights in October that year that Charles was wrongly accused of cheating. An argument broke out; both Thomas and Charles were set upon. Charles came off worse. One of the men had a knife, and he was killed."

All the while Richard had been speaking, Yvette was visualising the scene with Thomas, Charles and the other men standing around a table arguing. Then a fight breaks out. Charles is stabbed, his assailant flees, and Thomas kneels over the body of his friend, shocked and saddened by the outcome, his own face injured from the fight, whilst the other men stand around looking at the body. "What happened to Thomas?" asked Yvette.

Richard picked up his cup and took a drink, then continued. "He soon recovered from his physical injuries, but couldn't shake off the feeling of loss he felt for his friend. Not long after that his mother died, and Thomas decided to leave Shearwater for a while. He went to France and returned some months later, married to a French girl. She was, by all accounts, a beautiful young woman named Catherine, from a good and wealthy family, by the name of Dumont. They owned vineyards around Bordeaux, which had amassed their wealth. It had been a whirlwind romance, but the love Thomas and Catherine had for each other was plain to see. After that, Thomas was a changed man. Parties were held here again, which was something that hadn't occurred at Shearwater for a long time. Catherine was liked by everyone. It seemed Thomas was happy at last." Richard put his cup and saucer down, walked over to the settee, sat down, and went on with the story. "Then more trouble began. They had been married almost eighteen months when Catherine lost her first child in the early stages of pregnancy."

Yvette looked saddened, as Richard continued:

"They weathered that storm, and grew even closer. Then a few months later there was a bad fire here. Apparently, it had started in the kitchen, and affected most of the downstairs rooms. The upstairs wasn't too bad, but was smoke damaged."

Yvette thought of the flames licking the walls and ceilings, the furniture and curtains. She imagined people running around in panic, trying to help. "It must have been in ruins," she said.

"So much so," continued Richard, "Thomas and Catherine decided to return to her family in France, until repairs had been carried out. Apparently, most of the family portraits had been either destroyed or damaged, so before they left, it was arranged that on their return they would have their portraits painted together. Thomas insisted that any paintings saved from the fire should not be rehung until their portrait was finished and hanging in the manor. And with that they departed for France. They were there about three months when dreadful news was received: Catherine had been killed in a riding accident. She'd suffered a terrible head injury and died later that night."

"Oh, how dreadful," said Yvette, shocked and saddened by what she had just heard.

"Yes," said Richard, getting up from the settee and walking to the drinks cabinet. He held up a glass enquiringly to Yvette, but she shook her head. He poured himself a drink then went back and sat down on the settee again. Yvette was looking at the portrait.

"Yes, it was a bad business," said Richard. "She was buried in France, which was where I had been the morning I met you." He took a drink. "Thomas did all he could to bring her body back to England, but it wasn't possible. He returned home, and at first appeared to have taken it all very well. Then he did something very strange. One day he ordered an artist to be brought to the manor. He wanted the portrait to go ahead as planned. He said he would be painted standing beside a chair, so each time he looked at it he could imagine Catherine sitting there. Soon after completion of the portrait, came periods of deep melancholy. He lost all interest in himself and the manor. Almost four months after the death of Catherine he was found dead in the woods nearby. He'd shot himself."

"I didn't realise they'd both died so tragically, and so young," said Yvette sadly.

"Thomas was 29 when he died, Catherine just 23."

"That's my age," said Yvette, shocked at the injustice of it. She got up and walked over to the French windows, her arms clasped about her as if she were cold. She stared out of the window.

"Come on, darling," said Richard, trying to comfort her. "It all happened a very long time ago."

"Yes, I know," she replied, "but it doesn't make it any less sad."

The weather had been quite fine earlier, but now dark clouds were gathering and a storm was brewing. Already the distant rumble of thunder could be heard. Just then her attention was taken by some movement in the parkland beyond. Yvette noticed a man standing there, in the distance. She turned to Richard. "Who is this man?" she asked.

"What man?" asked Richard.

"He's just standing there looking across at the house."

Richard walked over to her and looked out. "Where?"

Yvette turned to look out again, but the man was gone. "There was someone..." she said.

"Well, there's no one there now," replied Richard, walking back and sitting down again.

"I wonder who it could have been," said Yvette.

"One of the gardeners I expect, wanting to catch a glimpse of the prospective lady of the house."

Yvette smiled as she sat down beside him.

"That's better," said Richard brushing her cheek with the back of his hand. After a moment they kissed.

# Four

That evening in the dining room, the wind was blowing the rain hard against the windows, which had their curtains drawn against the weather. A log fire burned brightly, and Richard and Yvette were seated at the dining table. They had just finished their meal and Richard was having a brandy. He took out a cigarette and lit it, blowing the smoke out, deep in thought. Yvette was looking across at him, smiling.

"You look very thoughtful," she said. "Is it anything I can share?"

Richard smiled back at her. "I was just thinking what a surprise the Applebys will have when I tell them I'm engaged to be married. I haven't told them yet; I want it to be a surprise."

"The Applebys?" enquired Yvette.

"Yes, Reginald and Barbara. Remember I told you about them when we were in France? They live at Flaxted Hall, a couple of miles from here."

"Oh yes," remembered Yvette. "You want them to come to the wedding."

"More than anyone else," replied Richard. "Present company excepted, that is." He took a pull on his cigarette. "They were close friends of my parents, and treated me like a son, especially after their deaths, which is more than I can say for my relatives." He took a drink, then continued. "When I first bought this place, they offered moral support and advice on many a dark, depressing evening, when I thought I'd bitten off more than I could chew. I don't know what I would have done without them. They'll be as pleased as punch about you."

"They sound very nice," smiled Yvette.

"Yes, they are. They'd help anyone who needed it. They're mad about horses, as well. If ever you needed any advice, you wouldn't go far wrong asking them. Which reminds me: remember the smart riding gear I bought you in France?"

Yvette smiled apprehensively. "Yes."

"Well, it wasn't just for show, you know, although it did look rather good on you. Would you fancy an early morning ride? Tomorrow morning, perhaps?"

"I don't know," replied Yvette doubtfully. "I did tell you, I've never ridden before."

"You'll be perfectly safe with me," he said. "I'll have Benson saddle up old Bonny – she's a quiet, docile mare – and we can have a nice amble down the lanes and through the woods. What do you say?"

"Well, I suppose that would be all right," said Yvette, though still uncertain.

"Splendid," said Richard, pleased. "Well then, that's settled. Tomorrow you shall have your first riding lesson." He heard the rain outside. "Weather permitting that is." He took a pull on his cigarette. He didn't notice her expression of apprehension. "By the way," he continued, "what do you think of your bedroom? It's really only a guest room, but I hope it will do for now."

Yvette smiled as she absently folded her napkin. "It's very nice, thank you."

"You don't have to do that, you know."

"What?" asked Yvette.

"Fold your napkin. There's really no need. Maurice sees to all that."

"I'll never get used to being waited on," she replied.

"Of course you will," said Richard, stubbing out his cigarette. "You should enjoy it."

"Yes, I suppose so."

Richard finished his drink, got up and walked over to the fire. He picked up a poker and poked at the logs. They flared up and crackled. As he replaced the poker he said, "You know, all the time I was in France I missed this old place." Yvette got up and walked over to him, and linked her arm with his. "I couldn't wait to get back," he continued. "Yet now I am back, I feel as though I've never been away; as though the trip to France was just a dream." He looked at Yvette and smiled. "A beautiful dream, where I met you."

Yvette rested her head against him. "I'm so happy, Richard. Let's promise ourselves we'll never leave."

He looked at her. "Not even for a holiday?"

"Well, maybe just for a holiday," she smiled.

# Five

In her bedroom that night, Yvette was standing by the slightly open window, overlooking a garden of red roses in such profusion their scent filled the air. The rain had stopped, and she took a deep breath and closed her eyes. It was so beautiful, she felt she needed to take in the moment. Then she turned to get changed into her night attire. The room was neither masculine nor feminine, to suit a man or woman, or both. As Richard had said, it was a guest room, beautifully decorated and tastefully furnished. There was a double bed, with bedside tables either side, on which were placed electric lamps, a candle in a holder on each, and a box of matches. Yvette was perplexed. Why candles when they had electric lamps? There was also a jug of water and a glass. A large mahogany wardrobe and matching set of drawers were against one wall; a dressing table with a seat stood in a corner of the room, on which Yvette had already placed her brush and comb set. There was a fireplace (the fire ready to light if need be), and an ornate clock on the mantel.

Some time later Yvette was asleep in bed. The rain had started again, there was a flash of lightning through the partly drawn curtains, and a few seconds later a rumble of thunder. Yvette was dreaming. She was in a wood riding a grey horse. They were cantering along a track between the trees. The sun was glinting through the high branches overhead. Her dream was peaceful and she was enjoying it. But then she heard something rustling in the bushes a little way off. She reined in her horse and stopped. She looked around, then heard a loud bang. Her horse reared and she fell to the ground.

She woke suddenly and sat up in bed, deeply disturbed by her dream. She reached out to turn on the lamp, but nothing happened. Then she remembered the candle and felt around for the matches. So that was the reason they were there, probably a regular occurrence during a storm. She lit the candle, got out of bed and put on her lace-trimmed negligee.

She opened the bedroom door and stepped into the corridor. There were several doors, with one on its own at the end. Yvette turned and walked towards the staircase, and stepped slowly down the stairs.

Lightning flashed through the large window above the stairway, lighting for a couple of seconds the hallway below. Then there was a loud clap of thunder. Yvette carried on down the stairs, her candle flickering, making large shadows on the walls. She walked across the hallway and into the sitting room. She made her way to the drinks cabinet and placed her candle on it. But before pouring herself a small brandy to steady her nerves after her nightmare, she opened the curtains slightly and looked out. Just at that moment there was a flash of lightning, illuminating the whole garden, and she thought, only briefly, that she saw a man standing at the far end of the lawn. She was afraid. She wasn't sure if she'd seen someone or if it was her mind playing tricks on her. Then there was another flash, but this time Yvette could see no one.

She felt relieved as she closed the curtains, then turned to the cabinet and poured herself a drink.

Suddenly, there was a great gust of wind and the French doors blew open. The curtains billowed into the room, and her candle was snuffed out. Yvette turned around quickly in fear, and stood trying to calm herself. After a few moments she pulled herself together. After all, it was only the storm. She closed the windows and drew the curtains together again. The room was now quite dark after her candle had blown out, but there was still a glow from the embers of the fire.

She was shaking as she took a sip of brandy, and walked to the settee and sat down. She leaned back and closed her eyes for a few moments. When she opened them again she was staring at the portrait, and Thomas's face dimly lit by the dying embers of the fire. She took a sip of brandy, then heard footsteps walking across the hall towards the door. She was afraid as she heard the steps getting closer and closer, then heard the doorknob slowly turning. She stood up quickly and turned towards the door. It slowly opened, and in came Maurice, in his dressing gown, holding a candle.

Yvette was relieved. "Oh, Maurice, it's you," she smiled.

"Yes, miss. Is everything all right?"

"Yes, thank you," replied Yvette. "I just came down for a nightcap. I had a bad dream."

"Oh, I see." He looked around the room. "Only I thought I heard something."

"That would be the doors," she smiled. "They blew open."

Maurice walked over to check them. "How strange," he said. "They've never blown open before. I'll have to see about having a stronger lock fitted." He smiled kindly at Yvette. "Can I get you anything, miss, whilst I'm here?"

"Oh, no thank you. I'll just finish this and then I'll be going back to bed." Suddenly she remembered her candle had blown out. "If you could just light my candle again, I would be grateful. It's on the drinks cabinet."

"Certainly, miss." He walked over to the candle, lit it from his own, and took it over to Yvette.

"Thank you, Maurice."

"Not at all, miss. I'll bid you goodnight." And with that he left the room.

The wind was still battering the rain against the windows as Yvette walked towards the door. Just before she left the room she turned and looked around, her eyes coming to rest again on the portrait. She stared at it for a few moments, then walked out.

# Six

Next morning the sun was trying to break through a haze of mist, which hung over the rose garden. Yvette looked out. It was going to be a fine day.

Some time later she was seated at the dining table, halfway through her breakfast. Then Richard entered the room, having left a little time before to take a phone call. As he took up his napkin again he said, "That was David Jennings, the vicar, on the phone."

"Oh, what did he say?" asked Yvette eagerly.

Richard looked at her and smiled. "Everything is set for 29 September."

"Oh, Richard, how wonderful. Morning or Afternoon?"

"11.15 in the morning. Oh, and he'd like to see us both some time."

"Why?" asked Yvette.

Richard took a sip of coffee. "Nothing to worry about. He wants to meet you, and to discuss the arrangements. I said we'd drop over one afternoon."

"Oh, I see."

"I'll have to ring the Applebys to see if the date will be all right with them. I tried last night, but they were out. I was hoping to have heard from them this morning, before I rang David to confirm." He lit a cigarette. "I'll try them again after breakfast, before we go for our ride."

Yvette became solemn and looked down, playing with her food. Oblivious to this, Richard carried on:

"There won't be much to do, thankfully. I told David it will be a very quiet affair; neither of us have any close family to consider. I'll just send out a few invitations to friends." Suddenly he noticed Yvette was looking troubled. "Darling! Is something wrong?"

Yvette smiled. "I'm not sure I should go riding this morning."

Richard picked up his coffee cup. "Oh, why not?"

Yvette felt silly, then decided to tell him. "I had a bad dream last night. I dreamt I was out riding; there was a loud noise, like a gunshot. My horse reared and I fell."

Richard stared at her for a moment, coffee cup in hand. "Then what happened?" he asked.

"I woke up," she replied.

"Then I shall have to take extra special care of you, won't I? Anyway, I've asked Benson to saddle up Bonny. She's the horse I learned to ride on, with the help of the Applebys. She really is quite safe, or I wouldn't chance it."

"It frightened me, Richard. In fact, I came downstairs and had something to drink to calm my nerves."

"Poor darling. I suppose it's my fault."

"Your fault? Why?"

"Telling you about Thomas yesterday, and how his wife was killed in a riding accident."

"Oh yes," said Yvette thoughtfully. "I suppose it could have been that." After a pause she continued. "I felt a little embarrassed. Maurice came in."

"Oh, why was that?"

"The French windows blew open in the storm, and he must have heard it. He came to see what had happened."

"Good Lord, he must have sensitive ears. I never heard a thing."

"He frightened me actually, at first."

"Maurice frightened you? Why?"

"I was sitting in front of the fire with my drink when I heard footsteps slowly approaching the door." She shivered at the memory of it. "It was so eerie."

Richard was a little amused. "You don't believe in ghosts, do you?"

Yvette didn't want to answer his question. She thought he was making fun of her, so she started to butter her toast.

"Do you?" repeated Richard.

Yvette looked across at him. "There were no lights – the storm must've brought a line down somewhere. Luckily I'd noticed a candle on my bedside cabinet earlier."

"Yes, Maurice always makes sure there are candles handy when there's a storm brewing. We've had the lights go out on us before."

Yvette wiped her fingers on her napkin. "Even that went out when the doors blew open. And then hearing those footsteps approaching the door... As I said, it was all so eerie."

Richard took a pull on his cigarette and leaned back in his chair, watching her. She did look troubled and he softened towards her. "You needn't worry, you know."

"What?" asked Yvette.

"This house. It isn't haunted, despite its tragic history. And anyway, I don't believe in all that, and neither do you, if truth be told." He smiled warmly, trying to make her feel better.

Later that morning Yvette was standing in the hallway, dressed in her riding clothes, waiting for Richard. Then he came into the hallway, also dressed for riding.

"Is everything all right?" asked Yvette.

"I've been trying to ring the Applebys but I can't get through. There must be a line down somewhere after the storm." He put on his riding gloves. "Oh well," he continued, "I'll try again later. Come on, let's go for our ride. We'll walk round to the stables. I'll introduce you to the horses, and Benson, of course."

# Seven

They chatted as they walked to the stables. Yvette was a little concerned. "You don't think there'll be a problem with the Applebys coming to the wedding, do you? I know how important it is to you."

"I hope not. I just wish I could've got through to them last night, before the line went down." He was thoughtful as they continued towards the stables. "Tell you what, we'll drive over there this afternoon. I want to introduce you to them anyway."

"I hope they approve of me," smiled Yvette.

"Don't worry, darling, they will." He gave her a peck on the cheek and put his arm lightly around her waist as they walked into the stable yard. There were eight stables, but five of them were shut. The yard was cobbled, and wheelbarrows and pitchforks leant against the walls. There was the smell of sweet hay and straw. A man in his 40s came out of one of the stables to greet them, leading a beautiful bay horse of around 16 hands.

"Good morning, Benson," said Richard. "How are you?"

"Can't grumble, thank you, sir."

"This is my fiancée, Miss Moreau."

Benson smiled and lifted the peak of his cap. "Good morning, miss."

"Good morning," replied Yvette, smiling.

"I see you've tacked up Sultan for me," said Richard as he patted the horse's neck.

"Yes," replied Benson. "'Ee's a bit full of himself this morning."

Richard took from his pocket a lump of sugar and gave it to the horse, who crunched it up in no time.

"He's beautiful, Richard," smiled Yvette.

"Yes. He's the finest horse around these parts, in my opinion," said Richard. "But don't tell the Applebys I said so."

Just then, the young stable boy, Joe, came out of another stable, leading a grey horse.

"The roan is for you – Bonny," Richard said, turning around as the stable boy approached them, then curiously, he looked at Benson. "Just a moment: this isn't Bonny."

"No, sir. Bonny came up lame this morning, so I saddled up Moonwind. She's a bit more spirited, but I'm sure Miss Moreau will 'andle 'er all right." He turned and smiled at Yvette.

Richard was concerned. "Well, I don't know about that. She's never —"

Yvette overcame her nerves, and interrupted. "I'll be all right, Richard, please don't fuss. And anyway, you'll be with me."

"All right then," he said, "if you're sure." He led her to the horse, and as the stable boy held the bridle, Richard helped Yvette into the saddle. He made adjustments to the girth and stirrups, and showed her how to sit and hold the reins. He looked up at her and smiled. "Comfortable?"

Yvette smiled nervously at him and nodded her head.

Richard squeezed her knee. "Don't worry," he said, "we shan't be doing anything faster than a walk this morning, and I'll be right beside you."

Yvette felt reassured as Richard walked over to the other horse. Benson helped him to mount. He adjusted the girth, then looked across at Yvette. "Come along then," he smiled. Yvette nervously urged the horse on, and they moved off as Benson looked on. Then he and the stable boy returned to their work.

As they walked along the quiet country lane, Yvette started to feel better. Richard was pleased. "Enjoying it?" he asked.

"More than I expected," she said.

"That's the ticket. We'll make a horsewoman of you yet. It'll be a nice hobby for you, especially when I'm working."

Yvette smiled. "I'm going to need a hobby, am I?"

"I'm afraid having my own business can often be quite time-consuming. I wouldn't want you to be bored."

"I see," smiled Yvette.

"At least I've got good staff at the office – hardworking and trustworthy – otherwise I would never have taken time off to go to France, researching for my book. Just think, I would never have met you." He smiled across at Yvette. What a sobering thought."

Yvette smiled across at him as she continued to enjoy the ride.

Just then, a car passed them and both horses became unsettled. "Whoa, good girl," said Yvette nervously. It hadn't been totally lost on her that the horse she was riding was a grey, just like in her dream. Richard's horse, Sultan, had bucked and was tossing his head.

Richard could see Yvette was worried. He leaned over to her horse, took the rein nearest to him, and reined in both horses. "It's all right, she'll settle down," he said, trying to calm her.

"I'm all right, Richard," said Yvette, trying to allay her nervousness.

"We'll be in the wood soon," he said. "It's just up ahead. It'll be quiet there this time of the morning, and we'll be off the road."

"As long as you think it's safe," she said, thinking again of her dream.

Richard smiled. "Of course it is." He released his hold on her horse.

They rode on a short while then turned off and walked into the wood along a wide track. But as they rode, someone was watching from the trees…

"This is better," said Richard. "No cars, and just a nice amble, like I said."

Yvette smiled at him, trying her best to overcome her nerves. They rode along chatting, then saw two figures in the distance: a woman on a horse, and a man who had dismounted and was holding up and inspecting one of his horse's feet. Richard reined in his horse, as did Yvette.

"What is it?" she asked.

Richard looked ahead and gradually he smiled. "I don't believe it, what a stroke of luck." He looked at Yvette. "It's the Applebys." He urged his horse on. "Come on, I'll introduce you."

The Applebys turned as they heard them approaching. Yvette guessed they were both in their late 50s, dressed in smart riding clothes. Reginald Appleby straightened up and smiled.

"Well I never," he said. "Richard, it's good to see you. I tried to phone you this morning. Blasted phone out of order."

"Yes, I know," replied Richard. "I couldn't get through either. How are you both?"

"We're fine, Richard. It's lovely to see you again," smiled Barbara Appleby. "When did you get back from France?"

"Only yesterday," he replied. "And I have a wonderful surprise for you both. May I introduce you to Yvette Moreau, my fiancée?"

"Oh, Richard, you don't mean it!" said Barbara, shocked but very pleased. "How perfectly splendid."

Reginald smiled, surprised at the news. "Your fiancée. Well, well. It's about time, I must say." He walked over to Yvette, taking off his riding glove, and shook hands with her. "I'm very pleased to meet you, Yvette."

She smiled at him. "How do you do?"

Barbara smiled her congratulations. "I'm so happy for you both. I thought he would never settle down." She looked at Richard. "When did you get engaged? We heard nothing about it."

"Two weeks ago, in France," smiled Richard.

"Oh, how romantic," said Barbara. "Have you set a date yet for the wedding?"

"Yes we have, and it's a piece of luck meeting you here like this, because we want to know if you have anything planned for 29 September? That's three weeks away."

"Well if we have, it's nothing that can't be cancelled. Isn't that right, Regi?

"Absolutely, old girl."

"What a relief," said Richard.

"Richard was so anxious to have you with us on our wedding day. That's why we didn't get married in France."

Barbara was touched. "Oh, Richard, how very thoughtful of you. We wouldn't miss it for the world."

"And you'll be my best man, Regi?" asked Richard.

"Of course I will, old boy. I'd be delighted."

"Oh, I say," said Barbara. "Isn't it exciting?" She looked across at Yvette. "But what about your family, my dear? Will they be coming over?

"Yvette has no family," explained Richard.

"Oh, I see," said Barbara. "I'm so sorry, I didn't mean to pry."

Yvette smiled weakly. "Please don't worry about it."

"Well, now that's settled, would you care to ride along with us?" asked Richard.

"Why not?" answered Regi. "Just give me time to hoist meself up into the saddle."

The four of them rode along, chatting, Reginald and Richard at the front, and Yvette with Barbara behind.

"D'you think you'll like it here in England, Yvette?"

"Oh yes, it's so beautiful," she replied. "And everybody is so kind."

They continued to ride along. Richard turned around to say something to Barbara and she urged her horse towards him. Yvette was a little way behind. Suddenly, there was complete silence. Yvette looked ahead. The others were chatting, but she couldn't hear them. There was nothing – no bird song or trees rustling in the breeze. She stopped, but the others carried on a few paces. She glanced over her shoulder and saw a man standing a little way off, behind her. He was handsome, but unkempt, his dark hair untidy. He was wearing breeches, black shabby boots to his knee, and a dirty white shirt. His face was unshaven. She stared at him for a few moments, then turned towards the others who had stopped a little way ahead and were calling her. But she could not hear them.

Suddenly, the sound returned: the birds, the rustling of the trees, and the others calling her, and asking what was wrong. She turned back towards the man, but he had gone. Meanwhile, Richard had turned and ridden back to her.

"What's wrong, darling?"

Yvette could not reply for a moment. Her heart was racing and her mouth was dry. Then after a moment she replied, "I thought I saw someone."

Richard looked around. "There's nobody here except ourselves."

Yvette looked behind her again. "There *was* someone," she said.

"Well, whether or not, they've gone now. Come on." They rode back to join the Applebys again, who both looked concerned.

"Is everything all right?" asked Barbara.

Richard smiled. "Yes. Yvette thought she saw someone, that's all."

"Oh," replied Barbara. "Are you all right, my dear? You've gone very pale."

"Yes, I'm fine thank you," smiled Yvette.

They began to ride on.

"Actually," said Richard, "would you mind if Yvette and myself took a shortcut home? It's the first time she's ridden, and I think it's enough for today."

"Of course we don't mind," said Barbara.

"Why don't you come back with us for lunch?" asked Richard.

"We'd love to," answered Barbara, "but we've got people coming over this afternoon, so we've got to get back anyway. It's been lovely to meet you, my dear, and you look natural on a horse. Keep it up. It really is the best thing in the world."

Yvette smiled at them both. "I've enjoyed meeting you, too."

"You must come over for dinner some time," said Richard.

"Love to," answered Reginald. "Anyway, look after yourself and your beautiful bride-to-be. 'Bye for now." The Applebys moved off.

"Come on," said Richard softly, "let's get you home."

Some time later they were in the dining room having their lunch. Richard had finished his meal and had coffee in front of him. But Yvette was toying with her sweet.

"Don't eat it if you don't want to," said Richard, a little concerned. "You've been very quiet since we got back from our ride, and you hardly touched your meal. Is anything wrong?"

"I'm just not very hungry, that's all."

After a moment he continued. "Now we've seen the Applebys and the date is OK for them, what say we drive over to the vicarage this afternoon?"

"Yes, I'd like that," she replied. Just then Maurice walked in to take their plates. Yvette looked at him apologetically. "I'm sorry, Maurice. Please tell Mrs Worth her meal was very good. I'm just not very hungry."

"That's all right, miss," he replied kindly. "Would you like me to get you something else?"

"No thank you," smiled Yvette.

Maurice took the plate away from her. "Will there be anything else, sir?"

"No, thank you," replied Richard.

"Very good, sir." And with that he left the room.

"You don't have to apologise to the servants, you know. It's nothing to them if you leave your food."

"I know! I just didn't want to offend Mrs Worth, that's all," replied Yvette, sharply.

Richard was taken aback. "All right, darling, I'm sorry."

Yvette stood up. "If you don't mind, I think I'll go up to my room now. If we're going to the vicarage, I'd like to change."

"Yes, all right, darling. I'll wait downstairs."

Yvette left the room. Richard lit a cigarette and slowly blew the smoke out. He looked thoughtful, wondering why she had snapped at him.

In her bedroom Yvette went to her bedside cabinet. There was a jug of water and a glass. She poured some water out, then walked over to her dressing table and took a bottle of aspirin out of the drawer. She took a couple of tablets, then sat on the stool before the mirror, and rested her head in her hands. After a moment she looked up and stared at her troubled reflection. Then she changed her clothes and went down to Richard who was standing in the hallway reading a newspaper. As she came down to him, he folded the paper and smiled at her.

"All set?"

"Yes," she answered.

He took her arm and they walked outside. The car was ready for them and Richard opened the door for Yvette to get in. Then he walked round to the driver's side and got in, throwing the newspaper on to the back seat. He turned on the engine and the car moved away down the drive.

Some time later, the car was parked just outside the vicarage gate, Richard and Yvette having gone inside some time ago. Then the door opened, and they came out, together with David, the vicar. He was a man of about the same age as Richard, and very pleasant. They were talking and laughing as they walked down the path towards the gate.

"I'm sure you'll both be very happy," he said. "You must come again when my wife is at home. She'd love to meet you, Miss Moreau."

"Thank you," she replied. "I'd like that."

They all shook hands.

"My very best wishes to you both," he said. They thanked him and walked over to the car. "See you both in church on Sunday."

"We'll be there," said Richard, opening the car door for Yvette. Before he got in the car himself, he put his hand up to wave.

As they drove off, Yvette turned to Richard. "He seems very nice."

"Yes, he is. He's done a lot of good work for the community. His wife is very nice too. It's a pity she was out, you'd like her. You must go round some time and meet her, as he suggested."

"Yes, I will," smiled Yvette.

They drove along the lane in silence, Yvette staring ahead of her. Suddenly she sat forward. "Can we stop,

Richard? I'd like to have a walk." He pulled the car over and they both got out. "It's such a lovely day," she said ecstatically, "it seems a shame to go straight back."

"Whatever you wish, my darling."

They linked arms and walked down the lane. It was narrow and winding with high hedges either side.

"I'm so happy, Richard. I can't believe it at times. A beautiful home, all this wonderful countryside." She stopped and looked lovingly at him. "And best of all, you."

He smiled at her and they kissed, then Yvette grabbed his hand and pulled him into a run. "Come on," she said, "let's go and stand by the bridge." A little further on, around a sharp bend, they came upon a stone bridge which crossed a small babbling brook. As they approached, Yvette let go of Richard's hand, ran over to the bridge and peered over the top. She turned to Richard. He was looking perplexed. "Let's find some sticks," she said enthusiastically, looking around on the ground. "We can throw them in the water and watch them come out the other side. I always loved doing that."

He smiled briefly, but watched her thoughtfully. Meanwhile, she had spotted a couple of sticks just behind him. "Oh, you're not looking, there's some behind you." She ran over and picked them up, then went back to the bridge and threw one of the sticks into the water. She dashed to the other side to watch it come through. "Here it comes," she laughed. "Look, Richard."

He walked slowly over to her and looked over the wall.

"There it is, see?" she said.

He stood looking over the bridge.

"Wait there," she said. "I'll throw another one." She did so then ran back again to Richard to watch it come out the other side. "There it is," she said excitedly.

Richard stood watching her. She looked at him, then stopped laughing. He smiled at her, but she sensed something was wrong. "What's the matter?" she asked.

"Nothing. Why?"

"You've gone very quiet. Do you want to go back?"

"No, it's not that," he said.

"Then it's me being silly, acting like a schoolgirl." She smiled. "I'm sorry, I've embarrassed you."

"Of course not," he replied.

"Then what is it?"

He looked at her a moment. "It's just that... Well, how did you know the bridge was here?"

"What do you mean?" she asked, perplexed.

"We couldn't see the bridge from where we were, but you knew it was here."

She looked away from him, thinking. "Oh, yes." She looked back at him. "I don't know. Perhaps I remembered passing it on the way to the vicarage."

"We didn't come this way," he said.

Yvette was puzzled. "How strange. I suppose I must have imagined it would be here. I mean, in the country there's bound to be a bridge over a brook somewhere, isn't there?"

He smiled at her, then put his arm around her shoulders. "Come on, let's get back to the car."

That night, Yvette was asleep in bed. She was dreaming she was back at the bridge where they'd been that afternoon, but she was alone, the wind rustling the leaves on the trees. Then she sees a man standing on the other side of the bridge with his back to her. Perplexed, she walks towards him. As she gets closer, he turns around. It is the man she saw that morning in the wood. She stops and stares at him.

She turned over restlessly in her sleep and continued to dream. This time she is in the wood where she'd been that morning, and the scene was repeated – she, mounted on the horse, looking back at the man she had seen – but now he walks towards her. Just before he reached her, she woke up suddenly, her eyes wide open as she stared into the darkness.

Next morning she walked into the dining room for breakfast, a little late. Various dishes, coffee and tea were set up on the sideboard. Richard was just finishing his meal.

"Good morning, darling," he said brightly.

She smiled a little sheepishly. "Good morning. I'm late, aren't I? I'm so sorry."

"Don't worry about it. It's for you to make your own time. This is your home now, don't forget."

Yvette poured herself a cup of coffee. "Not quite yet," she smiled as she walked over to the dining table.

"Just a formality," smiled Richard, then after a moment, "I hope you're going to have a little more than coffee for your breakfast."

"I'm all right, Richard, I'm not very hungry."

"You must eat, darling. You didn't have much yesterday."

"Yes, all right, I'll try a little something." She went to the sideboard, and lifted the lids on the various dishes. After a moment she spooned some scrambled egg onto her plate, and went back to the table. Meanwhile Richard had got up, putting his napkin down on the table.

"I know this is going to be a frightful bore, darling, but would you mind if I did a little work at the office this morning? I've been away such a long time, I should show my face and do some catching up."

Yvette was disappointed, but understood. "No, of course not."

"I thought if I could make an early start, we could spend the afternoon together."

Yvette smiled. "Yes, I understand."

He gave her a peck on the cheek. "I'll not be too long. Have a walk, or a look in the library. There may be something there of interest to you."

"Yes, I will," she said.

He smiled as he left the room. "See you later."

Just then Maurice entered with a trolley to clear up. He was surprised to see Yvette still at the table. She was embarrassed because of her lateness, and he saw she hadn't taken very much to eat.

"Is everything all right, miss? Can I get you something else?"

"No, it's all right. I've had all I want, thank you." She dabbed her lips with her napkin and got up. "You may clear if you wish."

"Well, if you're sure, miss."

Yvette smiled and left the room. She stood for a moment in the hallway, not really knowing what to do. Richard had suggested the library. Perhaps she could find a book to read. She turned and walked towards one of the doors, believing it to be the library, but it wasn't. It was Richard's study. She turned to walk out again, but hesitated, then walked into the room and glanced around. There were cabinets along one side, an armchair placed by an unlit fire, various prints of country scenes on the walls, and an office chair and desk, on which lay a notebook, file and typewriter. There was also a telephone. The window overlooked the garden. She walked over to the desk and glanced down at some typewritten papers. It was a draft of part of Richard's book he was writing on the history of Shearwater Manor. He was presently working on the years when Thomas lived at the manor. She read down the page, and felt a chill when she saw he was now up to the point where Catherine came into Thomas's life. Suddenly she turned away, feeling uncomfortable. She shouldn't be prying. She walked towards the door, then stopped. It was going to be a book; other people would be able to read it. Surely just to look at a snippet wouldn't do any harm. She turned and went back to the desk, picked up the pages and began to read.

It began with Thomas and Catherine's meeting. She read down the page and turned over to continue. She couldn't tear herself away, and after reading a few pages she got to the point of Catherine's accident, and her subsequent death. It told how she was riding alone that day. There had been rumours Thomas and Catherine had quarrelled, and that was why she was riding on her own. Strange – Yvette had always thought she'd been riding with Thomas. It continued to say she was found by a search party who had been summoned to find her when she did not return. She was still alive when they found her, but seriously injured. Yvette thought of poor Catherine lying there, staring up into the branches waving in the sunlight above her. Was she in and out of consciousness? Was her horse grazing nearby after she had fallen? She read on. Catherine was taken back to the chateau, and a doctor was summoned, but it was

## THE PORTRAIT

no use. Yvette imagined her lying in bed, her parents and the doctor standing over her, and Thomas by her side, holding her hand. It was evening when she was found and lanterns would be lit in the room, perhaps a lone candle on the windowsill. Then when she passed away, the sobbing of her parents, and Thomas, stunned and hopeless clinging to her hand, tears running down his face. Yvette imagined looking down on the scene, with the little group around the bed, the candle on the windowsill flickering violently then going out. And through the window the moon shining brightly on to the roof of the chateau as the stars twinkled overhead.

Just then she was disturbed by a quiet cough. She turned, and felt herself blush as she saw Maurice standing there.

"Sorry to disturb you, miss. I noticed the door was open."

"Oh yes. I opened the wrong door. I was heading for the library." She felt embarrassed. What must he think, seeing her standing there, reading Richard's work?

"The library is next door, miss."

"Yes, thank you." She put the papers down and walked out of the room. Maurice closed the door behind her.

Later that day, Yvette was in the sitting room reading a book she had found in the library, and trying not to look at the portrait. It was warm with the fire being lit, and after a while she fell asleep. Some time later Richard came into the room, having just got back from the office, and saw her asleep on the settee. He went over to her and kissed her on the cheek.

Yvette woke with a start. "Oh, Richard!"

"Sorry, darling. Did I startle you?"

"Just a little. I was reading, but just couldn't keep my eyes open. Shall I ask Maurice to bring some tea?"

"No thanks, not for me. But you have some."

"No, I had a drink earlier."

Richard sat next to Yvette on the settee and kissed the back of her hand. "I'm sorry I was later than I planned. There's still quite a bit to get through, but I'd had enough for one day."

Yvette smiled at him. She wondered if she should tell him she had been in his study reading his manuscript. She was worried Maurice might tell him. But why should he? Then again, perhaps she should tell him, just in case. Richard was tired and was resting his head on the back of the settee. She looked at him a moment, then she decided.

"Richard, I hope you don't mind but I found myself in your study this morning. I thought it was the library. I'm sorry. And I hope you won't be angry, but I saw the manuscript on the desk, and I started reading it."

"You did, did you?"

"Yes," she replied sheepishly. "I only meant to have a quick look, but found it so absorbing I kept reading. Then Maurice walked in and saw me. I was really embarrassed."

"So you should be," said Richard in mock anger.

Yvette looked ashamed. "I'm so sorry."

After a moment Richard smiled. "I don't mind. I'm glad."

"Really?" said Yvette, relieved.

"It's going to be read by someone, some time. I can think of no one better to have a first glance at it than you."

"Oh, Richard, thank you. I felt I'd been prying into something that wasn't my business."

"What did you think of it?"

"It was interesting, but very sad. I didn't know Catherine had been riding alone that day. I thought Thomas would have been with her, but of course they'd argued."

"Yes. The poor man blamed himself for her death, saying if they hadn't argued she would never have gone out alone. No one will ever know exactly what happened that day. Apparently she was a very good rider, but these things do happen."

"You wrote that she was very accomplished. She designed her own wedding dress and was a fine pianist."

"Yes," confirmed Richard. "She also had a great fondness for roses, especially red ones. She and her father cultivated a rose which they named after her. It was said she and Thomas brought a few back here to Shearwater after their marriage, to start a rose garden. In fact, I had a rose garden made at the back of the house. You can see it from your bedroom window."

"Yes," said Yvette. "It's beautiful." She was thoughtful for a moment then said, "Thomas shot himself after her death."

"Yes, it was all so tragic. He was a broken man when he returned after her death. He was not too bad at first, but then gradually lost all interest in himself and the manor. He went missing one day – 21 January 1829, to be precise. There was a snowstorm, and when he didn't come home a search party was sent out. They were hampered by the heavy snow but searched into the night. Then his body was found in Chatham Wood."

"Was that the wood we were riding in yesterday?" asked Yvette.

"Yes, that's right."

Yvette was imagining how it would have been: snow-covered trees and woodland, thick snow coming down through the branches, quickly becoming deep underfoot; the lanterns the search party carried flickering through the trees, as they battled their way through the snow, calling his name. Then the shock of finding him quite lifeless, almost covered with snow.

Yvette shivered. "How terrible," she said, glancing up at the portrait.

"Come on," said Richard, noticing her sad expression. "Let's go for a walk. Maybe the rose garden. You've not been there yet, have you?"

"No," said Yvette, brightening. "That would be nice."

They linked arms and left the room. The fire crackled noisily under Thomas's portrait above.

The next morning at breakfast, Yvette was more cheerful, and had eaten quite well. Richard was pleased.

"Well, I'm glad to see you've finished a meal at last. Mrs Worth must have been getting worried."

Yvette smiled at him. "Yes, I was quite hungry this morning."

"Must have been that walk in the gardens yesterday." He finished his coffee then said, "Maybe we could go for a drive this morning. What d'you think?"

"Yes, if you like, that would be nice," she said.

Just then Maurice walked in. "Sorry to disturb you, sir, but there's a phone call for you from the office."

Richard stood up, dabbing his mouth with his napkin. "Oh blast. Excuse me, darling." He left the room with

Maurice. Yvette drank her coffee. After a few moments Richard returned. "I'm sorry darling, we'll have to postpone our drive. I'm needed at the office. Would you like to come with me? I could introduce you to my trusty workforce. They'd love to meet you."

Yvette did not really want the fuss of meeting more people just yet. She felt tired, having not slept too well. She had been looking forward to them spending the day together. "Would you mind if I didn't today? Maybe another time."

Richard was disappointed but didn't let it show. "All right, darling. As you say, maybe another time. I'm sorry to have to leave you again, but I suppose it can't be helped, it is my business after all." He looked at Maurice who had just walked in to clear the breakfast things. "Have the car brought around for me, would you, Maurice?"

"Of course, sir." He left the room.

Yvette got up and walked over to Richard. She gave him a hug and kissed him.

"I'll try not to be too long," he said, as they both walked out of the room, arm in arm. "I know I said that yesterday, but I promise I won't be late."

"Don't hurry," said Yvette. "I don't want you having an accident."

As they walked to the front door, he gave her a quick kiss, then took his hat, coat and briefcase from Maurice, who opened the door for him. He ran down the steps, got in the car (which had just arrived), and drove away. Yvette watched as the car moved down the driveway. Then she walked back across the hall and went upstairs to her bedroom. She was relieved to see the room had already been cleaned, and she went over to her bed and lay down, putting her arm across her face. Eventually, she fell asleep.

Some time later she awakened and lay there a moment, as if unsure where she was. She got up and walked over to the open window and looked down on the rose garden. Again the beautiful scent filled the room. It was a lovely day, so she decided to get some fresh air and go for a walk. As she moved away from the window, she had no idea that someone had been watching her from the garden below...

Downstairs, she saw Maurice just entering the sitting room with a vase of flowers. "Oh, Maurice," she said. "If Mr Anderson should return whilst I'm out, please tell him I've gone for a walk."

"Yes, miss," he replied, and continued on his way.

Yvette decided to go to the rose garden again, and walked around to the rear of the manor. She came across the walled garden first and went in, as she had with Richard the day before. Pleached pear and apple trees grew against the walls, but mainly vegetables were grown here. In the far corner stood a greenhouse containing grapevines. Outside, leaning against it, were a hoe and spade, with a wheelbarrow nearby. No one was around. She walked to another door on the far side of the garden, through which she and Richard had entered the rose garden the day before. The door creaked as she opened it and was the only way in and out. This garden was also enclosed by high hedges. Here were the roses, in such profusion it was almost a shock. The scent and colour hit her, as they had the day before. She walked along one of the narrow paved paths which ran between the beds. There were a couple of small statuettes placed at the end of the path, and behind them was a white painted garden

## THE PORTRAIT

seat. The scent of the roses so close at hand made her heady. She went over to the seat and sat down. She felt so consumed in the moment, she closed her eyes, listening to the birdsong and the hum of a lawnmower, somewhere in the outer gardens.

Suddenly, she could hear nothing – no sound at all. She opened her eyes and looked around. As she scanned the garden, she noticed a movement on the far side. She thought it was probably one of the gardeners. She got up and walked towards the door where she had come in, but it was closed and there was no one around. She pressed her ears with her fingers, but still no sound. Then suddenly it returned – the birdsong, the lawnmower – as it was before. Perplexed, she walked back to the seat, but as she neared it, she could see something had been placed on it. She walked slowly towards it and was surprised to find a red rose lying there. She picked it up and looked around. Then she smiled. Richard must have returned and he was playing a trick on her. That is whom she must have seen a few moments before. But where was he now?

She left the gardens and went back to the house. She walked across the hallway and looked in the sitting room, then the study and library. He wasn't anywhere to be seen. She walked into the dining room where Maurice was setting the table for lunch.

"Can I help you, miss?" he asked.

"Can you tell me where Mr Anderson is? I can't find him anywhere."

"Mr Anderson is not back yet, miss."

"But I just saw him in the rose garden."

Maurice was perplexed. "I'm sorry, miss. Shall I phone his office for you? Then you can ask when he may be returning?"

"Oh, no, Maurice, that's all right. I wouldn't dream of disturbing him at work."

"As you wish, miss," he replied kindly.

Yvette turned and left the room. She was thoughtful as she went upstairs to her bedroom. She put the rose down on her dressing table and sat on the bed, then she noticed her book on the bedside cabinet. She picked it up and went down to the sitting room. She glanced at the portrait. The dark eyes seemed intense. She'd not noticed that before. She started to read her book, but she kept thinking about the man she saw in the wood, and the presence she'd felt in the rose garden. After about 10 minutes she realised she hadn't taken in any of the book she was reading. She closed it and leaned her head back against the chair. Soon after she heard voices in the hallway. Richard was back. He came through the door just as she was getting up to greet him. He was carrying a beautiful bunch of chrysanthemums.

"Oh, Richard," she said, flinging her arms around him. "I'm so glad you're back."

He was surprised but pleased by her welcome. "Hello, darling." He kissed her. "I was as quick as I could be." He handed her the flowers. "Have you had a nice morning?"

"Thank you, Richard, they're beautiful," she said, then hesitated. "Yes, I had a walk in the rose garden again."

Just then Maurice entered the room. "Would you like some tea, sir?"

"That would be nice," said Richard. "Oh, and can you find a vase for these, please?"

Yvette handed him the flowers.

"Certainly, sir. Miss." He left the room.

They both went to the settee and sat down. Richard began to tell her about his morning, and an interesting author he had met for the very first time. Yvette tried to listen, but her mind kept wandering back to the rose garden and the man she'd seen in the wood. After a while, she realised Richard had stopped talking and was looking at her.

"You've not heard a word I've said, have you?"

"Oh, I'm so sorry, Richard."

"Is something worrying you?" he asked.

She thought for a moment, then decided to come straight out with it. "Is this house haunted?"

Richard looked incredulously at her, then smiled. "What?" Then seeing her worried face, he said, "No, of course not. What makes you say that?"

"It's just that two things have happened that I can't explain."

"Such as what?" he asked.

"I didn't want to tell you because I thought you'd laugh at me, but when we were out riding I saw a man. Remember, I stopped in the wood? I couldn't hear anything for a few moments, Richard, then when I turned around there was a man standing on the track. Then when I looked again, he'd gone."

"A man? I never saw anything and neither did the Applebys, otherwise they would have said something."

"It's not just that, Richard. When I was in the rose garden this morning, it happened again. Suddenly I couldn't hear anything, and there was someone there, across the garden, but when I walked over to where I'd seen him, he'd disappeared. When I went back to the seat, there was a rose lying on it."

"I see," he said, trying to understand. "It's probably easily explained."

"How?" she asked.

"Well, first of all, the man in the wood could've been a poacher. He soon disappeared because he thought he'd be in trouble. As for the rose garden, it was probably Benson or Joe. One of them must have found the rose lying on the path and picked it up, meaning to put it on the compost heap, then he forgot."

Yvette was not convinced but said, "I suppose so."

Then Richard looked seriously at her. "Actually," he said, "I didn't want to tell you this in case it frightened you."

"What?" asked Yvette anxiously.

"Well, rumour has it, there is a presence here. Although I've not felt or seen it myself, I believe it's a terrifying sight."

"What is it?" she asked nervously.

"Well, every night at midnight, footsteps can be heard walking across the hall, and the sound of someone moaning and groaning. It is said you can almost hear the sound of creaking bones. A door screeches open then closes. And he is gone. They say it is a terrible sight for anyone who lays eyes on him."

"Who?" asked Yvette anxiously. "Who is it?"

"Only Maurice in his night attire wending his way to staff quarters." He leant back and laughed.

Yvette was annoyed. "Oh, Richard, why are you trying to make fun of me?"

"I wasn't making fun of you, darling, I was just trying to make you laugh, to cheer you up."

"Well, you failed miserably." They sat in silence for a moment, then Yvette started to smile. "I suppose it was rather funny, but poor Maurice, he isn't that old. You make him sound decrepit."

"Only a bit of fun," he said. "I wouldn't hurt him for the world. But I must say it's good to see you smiling. You've been lost in thought lately."

"Yes, I'm sorry," she said. "I don't know why I'm like this. It's just... If only I knew who it was I'd seen."

Richard was getting tired of the subject. "Look, I thought we'd sorted all this out?"

"It's just that there's been so much sadness here," she said. "Especially Thomas and his wife. It's all so tragic. Maybe he's a restless spirit."

Richard got up, feeling annoyed. "I don't know about Thomas, but you're certainly making me restless. I wish I'd never told you about him. I've never heard such nonsense in all my life."

Yvette was shocked by his anger, then Maurice knocked and walked in with the tea trolley. He had obviously heard raised voices, and looked a little embarrassed, as was Yvette. Meanwhile, Richard had walked over to the fire, and stood with his back towards her.

"Shall I pour, sir?" asked Maurice.

"No, it's all right, Maurice," said Richard, calming down. "We'll do it, thank you."

"As you wish, sir," and he left the room.

Yvette got up and walked over to Richard. She put her arms around him. "I'm so sorry," she said. "I didn't mean to annoy you."

"And I didn't mean to shout," said Richard. "It's not been a very good day for us, has it?"

"No, it hasn't," agreed Yvette.

Richard took her hand and kissed it. "Perhaps we should forget all about it."

Yvette smiled. "Yes, I think we should." She walked over to the tea trolley and began to pour.

# Eight

That evening, at dinner, it seemed everything was all right again. They enjoyed their meal and were now having coffee.

"I thought I'd invite Barbara and Regi over one evening for dinner. What d'you think?" asked Richard.

Yvette smiled. "Yes. That would be nice. When?"

"Oh, I don't know. Perhaps Saturday, if that's all right with you?"

"That's fine with me," she answered.

"I'll have to check with them first, of course."

"You're very fond of them, aren't you?"

"Yes, I am," he replied.

After a moment she asked, "Would you have changed the wedding arrangements if they couldn't have made that date?"

He considered a moment. "Yes, I believe I would."

Yvette looked down at her coffee cup. She was a little disappointed. "Oh."

"Would you have minded very much?" asked Richard.

"I would have been disappointed, yes." Just then she winced in pain and held her hand to her head.

"All right, darling?" he asked, concerned.

"Yes, I'm all right. It's just my head's started aching." She looked across at him. "Would you mind if I went to bed? I'm so tired. The rest and a couple of aspirin may ease it before it gets too bad."

"Of course I don't mind, but you're not ill, are you?"

She got up from the table and Richard went over to her.

"No," she said, "it's just a headache. I'll be all right in the morning."

He took hold of her. "I'm sorry I lost my temper with you earlier. I do love you, you know." He kissed her, and she put her arms around him and rested her head against his shoulder. Suddenly, she couldn't hear anything. Richard was talking to her, but she could not hear him, nor the fire crackling. Not even the clock on the mantel. All was silent. She closed her eyes, but when she opened them she was looking towards the French windows. It was almost dark by now. Then her eyes grew wide in horror. The man she'd seen in the wood was standing outside, looking in on them. She said nothing. Her heart was beating so fast, it was a wonder Richard couldn't hear it.

"We will be happy, Yvette, won't we?" said Richard.

But Yvette could not hear him and was still staring at the windows. Richard took hold of her arms and moved her back.

"Yvette, what's the matter?" Richard turned to where her eyes were focused, but the figure had gone. He shook her slightly. "Yvette?"

Suddenly, the sounds returned, she was aware again, but felt dazed. "Oh, Richard."

He was worried as he supported her. "You are ill."

Yvette knew she must not mention what she had seen for fear of starting another argument. "Yes, I think I must be. I don't feel very well."

"Shall I call the doctor?"

"Oh no, please don't do that. I'll be all right, really. A good night's sleep will put me right."

"Come on," said Richard. "I'll help you to your room."

A little later that night, Yvette was in bed staring up at the ceiling. There was no light on, but her curtains were partly open and the moonlight was shining in. There was a faint knock at the door. "Come in," she said. Richard entered the room and walked over to her bed. She switched on her bedside lamp.

"I wasn't sure if you would be asleep," he said. "How are you feeling?"

"A little better, thank you," she smiled.

"Are you sure you don't want me to call the doctor?"

"No, I'll be all right in the morning. I just need a good night's sleep, that's all."

"Don't attempt to get up for church in the morning, if you don't feel like it."

"I'll be all right."

"If you feel the least bit ill in the night, be sure to wake me, and I'll call for the doctor."

"Yes, I will. Don't worry."

He went over to the door then turned and smiled at her. "Goodnight, darling."

"Goodnight," she said, as he closed the door. She switched off the light, leaned back on her pillows, and stared at the moonlight shining through the window. After a few moments she turned on her side, and tried to sleep.

Later that night, in the grounds of the manor, the branches of the trees were creaking in the breeze. Overhead, white clouds were moving across the starlit sky. There was a full moon, and in Yvette's bedroom it was still shining through the partially drawn curtains, which were moving in the breeze from the slightly open window. Suddenly, she awoke and turned onto her back, staring up at the ceiling. After a few minutes she faintly heard music playing. She was unsure and sat up in bed listening. It was piano music, Beethoven's *Moonlight Sonata*. She sat a while straining her ears to hear. Surely her mind was playing tricks on her. The moon was shining, which had put the idea of the music into her head. Was she hearing it, or imagining it? But after a minute or so, she knew it was definitely someone playing the piano. Richard perhaps? But why would he be playing in the early hours of the morning? And surely it wouldn't be Maurice. She got out of bed, put on her negligee, and left the room. She walked down the staircase and the music became louder. As the drawing room was the only room with a piano, she walked towards the door. She felt nervous, but overcame it. It must be Richard. She turned the doorknob, and slowly pushed the door open. The music continued, but it wasn't Richard who was playing, nor was it Maurice. It was a woman, with her back to the door, playing as the moonlight streamed through the window, and by its light Yvette could see the woman had long dark hair. Her dress was certainly not of this era, and her body swayed as she continued to play. Yvette was terrified, yet she could not help herself. She walked slowly towards the woman. She was within a foot of her, then stopped and reached out to touch her shoulder. The music stopped, and as the head slowly turned, Yvette lost her nerve and ran from the room.

# THE PORTRAIT

In her bedroom, she rushed to the window and gasped at the fresh air. Soon she calmed down, but she was afraid. She stared out onto the moonlit garden below. The statuettes and the seat, where she had been sitting yesterday, stood out in the moonlight. But now she could see someone standing there – the man whom she saw in the wood, and who looked at them earlier through the dining room window. Yvette's heart was racing. Suddenly, he reached his arm up towards her, the hand of which held a red rose. Then he spoke.

"I love you, Catherine."

Yvette was stunned, her eyes grew wide and she made as if to scream. Suddenly she woke with a start, and sat up in her bed. As she realised it had all been a dream, she began to calm down. There was no moon, or music playing, but was there someone in the rose garden? She slowly got out of bed, and although not wanting to, she felt she must see if someone was there. She stood at the window and glanced down on the garden. With no moonlight it was quite dark. She could see the statuettes and the seat, but no one was there. She breathed a sigh of relief, walked back to her bed and turned on the lamp. She sat down and put her hand to her head, which had begun to ache. She took a couple of aspirin and sat down again. After a while she climbed back into bed, and lay there staring at the ceiling.

Outside someone was watching, as she turned and put out the light.

# Nine

Next morning, Richard and Yvette were coming out of church, after the service. The vicar, David Jennings, was standing at the entrance, shaking hands and talking to the congregation as they came out. Some of them nodded and smiled at Yvette and Richard, now knowing of their engagement and forthcoming marriage. He walked over to them.

"Nice to see you," he smiled, shaking hands.

"Good sermon this morning," said Richard.

"Short, you mean?" joked David.

They laughed, then David turned to Yvette. "And how are you, Miss Moreau?"

"Oh, please call me Yvette. I'm very well thank you."

Just then, David's wife came out of the church and walked towards them. She was a bit younger than her husband. She had a warm smile and was very pretty.

"Oh, Dorothy," he said, "just in time." He turned to Yvette. "May I introduce you to my wife, Dorothy?" Then he turned to his wife. "Darling, this is Miss Moreau, shortly to be Mrs Anderson."

They both shook hands.

"I'm very pleased to meet you, Miss Moreau."

"Please call me Yvette," she smiled.

"May I offer you both my congratulations?"

They both thanked her.

"Are you settling in at Shearwater, Yvette?" she asked.

"Oh, yes, thank you," she replied.

"It's a beautiful place, isn't it?" continued Dorothy.

But Yvette's smile had faded. She could no longer hear anything, and was staring across the churchyard at a figure standing by one of the gravestones. It was the man again, just as he had been the previous times she had seen him. He was looking across at her. Richard had noticed the change in her. He looked in the direction she was staring, but could see no one.

"Yvette," he said, and again, when she didn't respond, "Yvette!"

Suddenly she was aware again and could hear him. She looked bewildered as she turned back to them. "Oh, I'm so sorry. What were you saying?"

Both David and his wife looked perplexed, but Dorothy said again, "I was just saying, Shearwater is such a beautiful place."

"Oh yes, indeed," agreed Yvette.

Richard smiled. He was a little embarrassed. "I think we'd better be going," he said, "or we'll be late for lunch." He took Yvette's arm. "Come along, darling." Then to David and Dorothy, "It's been so nice to see you. We'll be here again next week."

They both smiled. "Goodbye, until next week," said David. He took Dorothy's arm and they walked back into the church.

"What was all that about?" asked Dorothy.

"I've no idea," answered David.

At the car, Richard felt annoyed as he held the door open for Yvette. She climbed in, then he went around the car and got in himself. He started the engine and drove down the road. After a few minutes Yvette sensed he was not very pleased.

"I'm so sorry, Richard. That was rude of me. It's just that—" She paused momentarily, a bit afraid to mention it again, but thought she must explain. "I thought I saw that man again. You know, the one I told you about."

"Yes, I thought that might be it," he said irritably. "It's not that surprising, is it? From the way you described him, he's probably a tramp living rough around here somewhere."

"Yes," she replied, unconvinced. "I suppose so."

They drove on and then, in an effort to break the atmosphere he said, "By the way, I rang the Applebys about dinner on Saturday. They said they'd be delighted to come."

# Ten

The next morning the rain was battering in and around the grounds of the manor. Inside Richard's study, Yvette was sitting in front of a roaring log fire, looking at the design of her wedding dress, which was being made by a dressmaker in the nearby town. Richard was at his desk going through the wedding invitation list. After a while Yvette got up, walked over to him and looked down at the list, whilst the rain battered against the window.

"Is there anything I can do?" she asked.

"No, it's all right, darling. I'm just going through the guest list to see who is likely to come and who isn't. The Applebys are a definite, of course, but I've tried to keep it to a minimum. It'll be too short notice for a lot of them anyway, I should think."

"It seems a shame," said Yvette.

"Not really. I only want things to be quiet. After all, you've none of your own friends and family coming."

"No," said Yvette solemnly.

Richard looked up at her. "I'm sorry, darling, I didn't mean to be insensitive."

She turned and walked over to the window, putting her hands across her upper arms, as if cold. Richard noticed this, then looked at the roaring log fire, then back to Yvette.

"Are you feeling cold?"

"Just a little," she said, watching the rain pouring down the window.

"Why don't you go and sit by the fire?"

"No, I'm all right."

"What's wrong?" asked Richard.

Yvette turned to him. "I feel so useless. All the arrangements being made for the wedding, and I seem to have no part in them."

"Don't think like that, darling. I just thought it would make things easier for you, that's all."

Yvette felt depressed, and turned back to the window again.

"The trouble is," he continued, "the weather can get you down this time of year. Yesterday it was beautiful. Now look at it."

"Yes," she replied.

Richard felt some sympathy for her. "I know it must be boring for you just now, but you'll soon make friends and find new interests. Remember we're going to Mrs Gilroy's tomorrow to see how your dress is coming along, and later we'll be going for your wedding ring, so you'll have a busy day."

"Yes," said Yvette, brightening. "I hadn't forgotten. I'm looking forward to it."

Richard turned back to his desk and started writing. "I thought we could go for a meal tomorrow evening, to round off the day. What d'you think?"

Yvette turned to him and smiled. "Yes, that would be nice."

Richard continued writing. "Oh, I meant to tell you: after tomorrow I'll be going into the office for the rest of the week. I want to sort out a few things before the wedding."

Yvette was disappointed. "Oh, I see." She continued to look out of the window. Suddenly the rain stopped, there was complete silence, and the sun was shining brightly. Yvette was shocked by the suddenness of it, and turned to Richard who was engrossed in what he was doing. There was no sound at all from the roaring fire or the clock on the mantel. She turned back to the window. At some distance she could see two figures, both in period dress. The man had dark hair and was dressed handsomely in breeches, white shirt and waistcoat. The woman with long dark hair, wearing a beautiful blue dress which was full from the waist and reached the floor. She could not see their faces as they were turned to each other, talking and holding hands. After a moment they kissed, then the woman pulled the man into a run, and they ran across the lawn, laughing. Yvette looked on in disbelief, then slowly turned to Richard. He was busy, but there was still no sound. "Richard," she said fearfully, but he could not hear her. Then all at once the sound returned, the rain battered against the window again, the fire crackled and the clock was ticking on the mantel. She turned back to the window, but now there was no one there.

Outside the manor, late that night, the rain had stopped, and clouds were racing across a starlit sky. Tree branches swayed and creaked, and in the distance a fox could be heard, barking. In Yvette's room, she was in bed reading a book. She hadn't been able to sleep, and the book wasn't really helping. Then suddenly she could hear a sound somewhere outside the room. The sound was muffled, but as she concentrated she realised, with some trepidation, it was a man sobbing. She listened intently, then got out of bed, put on her negligee and went over to the bedroom door. She opened it slowly. The sound was a little louder now, but she couldn't tell from where it was coming. After a moment she walked along the corridor towards Richard's bedroom, which was further on towards the staircase.

The only light was coming from her bedroom. The sound seemed to be getting fainter, and when she reached Richard's door, she put her ear to it, but it was not coming from there. She knocked lightly on the door. "Richard," she said softly. But Richard was asleep. Perplexed, she turned and walked back towards her bedroom, but now the sound was getting louder again. She passed her own door and walked on, the sobbing becoming louder as she approached a door at the end of the corridor. As she walked, the floorboards creaked, and the nearer she got, the more afraid she became.

Suddenly, the sobbing stopped. Yvette stood there not knowing what to do. She tried looking through the keyhole, but it had covers on both sides. Then she decided to look in the room. She turned the doorknob slowly, and pushed. Nothing happened – it seemed the door was locked. In a way she was relieved as she'd been afraid of what she might see. But still, the sound had been coming from within.

After a moment she turned and walked back to her bedroom. Before she entered she stopped a moment and looked towards the door again. All was quiet. She shivered, then entered her bedroom and closed the door.

Next morning the sun was shining brightly. There was no wind, and a mist hung over the gardens and parkland. Yvette opened her window and looked down at the rose garden. She breathed in the cool scented air. She was thinking about what had happened in the night, what or who it could have been, but she knew she couldn't ask Richard for fear of another argument.

Later that day, Richard and Yvette were in the town, coming out of the dressmaker's shop. Mrs Gilmore, the owner and manageress, had promised the dress would be ready in plenty of time. Yvette had designed it herself. It was kept quite simple, but it would be beautiful.

Richard was impressed. "I didn't know you'd designed your own wedding dress," he smiled. "You never showed me."

"I've been working on it for a while. I thought if Catherine can design her own wedding dress, then so could I." She smiled up at him. "I didn't show you because it's bad luck for the groom to see the bride's dress before the wedding day."

"Oh, I see," he smiled.

They walked on a few paces then suddenly Yvette asked, "Did you hear anything last night?"

"What sort of thing?" asked Richard.

"I don't know. It sounded like someone crying."

"Well, it wasn't me," joked Richard. "I've got nothing to cry about. The only other person it could be is Maurice, and he's on the other side of the house. He's got nothing to cry about either, but I suppose I could always give him a raise," Richard laughed. "It'll have been the wind playing tricks on you. I've heard it myself on occasions. It can sound strange, I know, but I shouldn't worry about it."

They arrived at the jeweller's shop and gazed through the window at the array of gold and silver rings, watches, and necklaces. They smiled at each other and went inside. From outside they could be seen looking at several trays of rings produced by the manager. They picked up various rings, and Yvette tried them on for size. Not long after, they left the shop with the most beautiful ring Yvette had ever seen.

That evening they were in a restaurant. It was very romantic as they were shown to a secluded, candlelit table. They enjoyed their evening, as they chatted easily to each other. Yvette was so happy. Now that her dress was in the process of being made, and the ring bought, she felt excited.

Richard took up a glass of champagne. "Here's to a long and happy future together. I love you, darling."

Yvette took up her own glass. "And I love you."

# Eleven

A couple of days later Yvette was beginning to feel more settled at the manor. She hardly thought of the man she'd seen in the wood and gardens, or the sound she'd heard that night, accepting Richard's explanation. It was only as she was seeing Richard off to work that it came back to her. They were standing on the steps at the entrance to the manor. Richard had his briefcase, and kissed her before putting on his hat. Then, walking down the steps to the car, he turned and said, "I don't really want to bring the subject up again, but have you seen that man at all since we talked about it?"

Yvette suddenly felt anxious, the reality of it coming back to her, but she answered, "No, I haven't." She tried to smile but her mind was racing and her heart began to beat faster.

"Well, if you do see him again, anywhere on our property, call the police."

"Yes, all right," she answered.

"Now promise me," said Richard.

Yvette felt irritated. "Yes, I've said."

"Good," said Richard. Then he opened the car door, throwing his hat and briefcase on the passenger seat before climbing in. Yvette watched him. She put her arms about her as if cold. Richard started the engine and looked through the side window and smiled at her, then he drove off. Yvette looked after him as he drove down the driveway. Her smile faded as she glanced over the lawns and parkland beyond. She felt a spot of rain and sighed, before turning around and walking back into the house, closing the door behind her.

She walked across the hallway, then suddenly, on impulse, she walked up the stairs and along the corridor to the room from where she had heard the 'sobbing' coming nights before. She moved towards it apprehensively. She tried the doorknob again, but the door was still locked. She stood there a moment, then heard something behind her. She swung around in panic, only to see Maurice standing outside Richard's room, carrying clean shirts. He looked a little alarmed at her standing there, as if he knew something he didn't want her to know.

"Is everything all right, miss?"

"Oh, yes thank you," answered Yvette.

Maurice stayed by Richard's door as Yvette, with a weak smile, passed him and walked down the stairs. Maurice looked at the door at the end of the corridor then, after a moment, went into Richard's bedroom.

Yvette walked into the sitting room and sat on the chair near the fire. After a moment she spotted a magazine on a nearby table. She picked it up and began to flip through the pages. It was a country magazine, more Richard's taste than hers. She put it down and went over to the windows. It was raining as she looked across the gardens. Suddenly, she felt she needed to get out. She was feeling uneasy again, which disappointed her after feeling so much better the last couple of days. She went to her room and got a raincoat from the wardrobe. It had a hood, and she put it up as she left the house, and walked around to the gardens. She came upon the walled garden again, but decided to take another direction. The lawns had just been mowed and she could smell the sweet cut grass. She walked along, deep in thought, the woodpigeons cooing in the trees and the birds singing. It was still drizzling, but a little brighter. She turned towards the house, which was some way off, and looked up. She realised she was looking at the windows of the room where she thought she had heard sobbing a couple of nights before. The curtains were drawn, so revealed nothing of the room within. She continued her walk, then suddenly found herself in overgrown, neglected gardens. There were larger trees and shrubs, ferns and overgrown grass. She realised she had left the main gardens, and looked about her. Just then the rain came down harder and she pulled the hood tighter around her head. She ran under one of the trees and stood there, looking about her. Then she noticed, some distance from where she was standing, a dilapidated summerhouse set amongst the overgrown shrubbery and trees. She was curious and made her way towards it. It was stone below, with timber, now rotted, up to the roof, which was now mainly open to the elements. It was very old and uncared for, a shell of what it had once been. There had been windows but the glass had long gone. She stood at the entrance for a moment, then walked slowly inside. It was very gloomy because of the rain and tree branches overhead, and the floor was littered with dead leaves, twigs, and debris from the rotting summerhouse. The rain was dripping through the gaping holes in the roof. She walked over to one side of the summerhouse where a window had once been, and looked out. After a few moments the rain became lighter, and a watery sun sent a shaft of light inside. Yvette thought of how it would have been in the past.

Suddenly she heard (or thought she heard) the whispering voice of a man. Was it her imaginings? She heard the voice say:

*"I love you, Catherine. I love you. Promise me we'll never part, for I could not live without you."*

Then there was silence. It had been her imagination, of course. She turned to leave, then saw a stone seat against one of the walls. It too was littered with leaves, but also, lying there, was a single red rose. She felt certain it hadn't been there when she came in. She walked over and picked up the rose, and breathed in its beautiful scent. Then she heard the snapping of a twig outside. She turned around nervously, but no one was there. Suddenly, she didn't want to be there any longer; there was a feeling of despair about the place. She walked out, then ran back to the house.

She walked hurriedly across the hall. No one was about. She ran to her room, closed the door and leant against it. After a few moments she walked over to her dressing table and placed the rose there. She took off her wet raincoat and draped it over a chair. She sat on her bed. Her head had begun to ache. She took a couple of aspirin, kicked off her shoes and lay on her bed. She didn't know how long she'd been there, but she suddenly woke up. Her headache had gone, and she sat up and glanced towards the dressing table. Then a look of disbelief clouded her face. She got up and walked slowly towards it. The rose was still there, or what was left of it, because it had crumbled to dust.

# Twelve

That night, outside the manor, there was a starlit, cloudless sky. An owl hooted nearby. There were various lights on inside the manor, and the carriage lamps were lit outside the door. Richard drove up to the house and got out of the car, carrying his hat and briefcase. He ran up the steps and was greeted by Maurice, who held the door open for him.

"Good evening, sir," he said.

"Good evening, Maurice," replied Richard.

Maurice took Richard's hat, coat and briefcase.

"I'm afraid I'm rather later than I expected. I hope Miss Moreau has eaten."

"No, sir," said Maurice. "Miss Moreau said she would prefer to wait for you. She's been in her room most of the evening."

"I see." Richard looked at his watch. "Well, in that case, I won't bother changing. We'll eat straight away."

"Very good, sir."

As Maurice walked away, Yvette ran down the stairs and across the hallway. "Oh, Richard."

He was pleased by her welcome, but rather surprised at her enthusiasm. "Hello, darling. I'm sorry I'm so late. Have you missed me?"

"Oh yes," said Yvette earnestly.

They kissed briefly, then Richard took her arm and they walked into the dining room. "What have you been doing with yourself all day?" asked Richard, as they took their seats.

"Oh, nothing much," smiled Yvette. "I went for a walk in the gardens." She looked away from him and stared across the room. She was thinking of the summerhouse, and her smile faded. It would be dark there now under the starlit sky; the ferns and grasses rustling in the light breeze, and the branches of the trees creaking. She thought what it would be like inside, and how mice and even rats would be scurrying across the floor, and maybe on to the stone seat where she'd found the rose. Suddenly she was interrupted in her thoughts by Richard speaking.

"Darling, are you all right?"

She turned to him and gave a weak smile. "Yes", she replied. "Yes, I'm all right."

Next morning, in the dining room, Yvette was half way through her breakfast, eating slowly. Richard had finished his and sat with a cup of coffee and a cigarette. He glanced at his watch. "I'll have to start out for the office in a moment, darling. Maybe then, I can be home a little earlier." He took a pull on his cigarette. "Don't forget, the Applebys are coming tonight."

"I hadn't forgotten," she said. She was thoughtful for a moment and then asked, "Richard, the summerhouse – has it always been there? It looks very old."

Richard had his coffee cup halfway to his lips. He thought for a moment. "The summerhouse? Oh yes, I know what you mean. Yes, it's in a bit of a state, isn't it? I imagine it's been there at least since Thomas's time. Why?"

"Can't something be done about it?" she asked.

"I think that part of the garden is due for some work. I could have it pulled down and another built in its place, if you like."

"Oh, no," said Yvette, alarmed. "No, please don't do that. Perhaps it could be repaired?"

Richard was surprised. "I shouldn't think so, there's hardly anything left of it." He finished his coffee and could see the anguish in Yvette's eyes. He was surprised she should care so much. "I'll have a word with Benson. He does the gardens as well as looking after the horses. I'll see what he thinks about it."

"Thank you," she smiled. She toyed with her food, not feeling very hungry. There was something else she wanted to ask but felt uneasy about it. After some thought she asked, "The room upstairs at the end of the corridor – what is It?"

"Just a bedroom," smiled Richard, stubbing out his cigarette.

"A guest room?" asked Yvette.

"Yes, that's right," answered Richard, feeling uneasy, not wanting to discuss it.

"I see. Only I noticed the door is locked," she said, a little hesitantly.

Richard looked concerned. "You tried the door?"

"Well, I knocked first, though I didn't think there'd be anyone in there. I just wanted a look inside, that's all."

"There's nothing in there of any interest. I keep it locked because—" He grappled for a reason. "Well, I have some private documents in there, that's all." He stood up, putting his napkin on the table.

Yvette was unconvinced. "I see," she said. She stood up as well but Richard said:

"It's all right, darling. You stay and finish your breakfast."

Yvette sat back down. Richard felt sorry for her. He went over to her, and gave her a peck on the cheek and smiled. "I won't be late, darling, I promise. It won't always be like this. It's just I have so much to catch up on, what with going to France and the wedding coming up." He walked to the door, then turned and said, "Why don't you go to the stables and see the horses? It looks like it's going to be a fine day."

"Yes, I might."

He opened the door then turned to her. "'Bye, darling."

"'Bye," she smiled. But as he closed the door her smile faded. She felt very alone as she heard the car start up and Richard drive away.

Later that day, Yvette decided to do as Richard had suggested. She walked around to the stables. The stable lad, Joe, was brushing the yard.

"G'day, miss," he said.

"Good day," smiled Yvette. She walked to one of the stables where Richard's horse, Sultan, had his head over the door. She began to stroke his face, then after a few moments she walked to another stable which had an older, roan horse looking over the door at her. Yvette stroked its face, then Benson came over to her, and touched the peak of his cap.

"G'day, miss."

"Good day," she smiled. "It's turned out rather nice, hasn't it? I thought I'd just come and have a look around." She felt a little self-conscious and turned back to the horse. "This horse has a kind face. What's its name?"

"Bonny, miss," Benson replied kindly, as he patted the horse's neck. "Yes, she's a good-natured mare."

"Ah, yes," remembered Yvette. "She was the one I was to have ridden that morning."

"That's right, miss. She'd come up lame. She seems all right now, though."

"That's good," said Yvette.

"D'you want to take 'er out, miss? I can 'ave 'er tacked up in the time it'd take yer to change."

"Oh, no thank you," she smiled, "not today. I just wanted a walk, that's all."

"Just as yer like, miss." He smiled as he lifted the peak of his cap. "G'day," and he walked away to get on with his work.

Yvette stood for a moment then turned and walked out of the stable yard. She glanced towards the place where she'd found the summerhouse the day before, but she didn't want to go there today. Maybe some time when she was with Richard, she'd visit it again, and perhaps Richard would have something done to repair it. She hoped so.

# Thirteen

That night, outside the manor, lights shone from many of the windows, and the carriage lamps were lit. The Applebys car was parked outside. In the dining room, Richard and Yvette were seated at either end of the table; the Applebys on either side. They were partway through their meal, and Maurice was attending at table. Yvette seemed a little subdued, a fact that hadn't gone unnoticed by Richard.

"That time away has certainly done you good, Richard. You look marvellously well," smiled Barbara.

"Yes, it had been some time since I'd been able to get away, what with one thing and another. But now I know I can leave the business in capable hands, it makes things a lot easier."

"You mean Michael Fotheringay?" asked Reginald.

"Yes. Father said he'd be an asset to the business, and he's certainly proved his worth." He took a sip of wine. "I'm thinking of offering him a partnership. Lord knows he deserves it." He patted his mouth with his napkin." But I'll wait until after the wedding, when things are little more settled." He smiled across at Yvette, but she was looking down at her plate. She'd hardly eaten anything. Richard's smile faded, wondering what was troubling her. He felt a little irritated too, thinking the Applebys would notice, but he continued with his meal.

"Done any more riding lately, Yvette?" asked Reginald.

She did not hear him, and Richard thought it best to intervene. "Yvette!" he said quite loudly.

She looked up. "Oh, I'm so sorry, what did you say?"

"I just wondered if you'd done any more riding," repeated Reginald.

Yvette smiled. "No, not since that day."

"Oh, you must, my dear," smiled Barbara. "Such a pleasant hobby to have, and the more you do it, the more confident you'll become."

"Yes, I suppose so," she replied.

"Well, you'll have plenty of time after the wedding. I suppose you're rather busy with arrangements at the moment?"

"No, not especially," replied Yvette. "Richard has done most of it. I've not been that involved."

"I told you, I just wanted to make things easier for you, that's all," said Richard. "It's been a big step for you, and a brave one, to come to another country. I wanted you to take your time getting used to the place."

Barbara sensed some tension had begun to develop. "Richard's right," said Barbara kindly. "To come to another country and to such a large house. I take my hat off to you, my dear, I really do."

Yvette smiled. "Yes, I suppose so. Thank you."

"It's such a beautiful house, isn't it?" continued Barbara. "So much history behind it. I expect Richard has told you of the tragic tale of Thomas and his wife, Catherine?"

"Yes," replied Yvette.

"Such a tragic story, don't you think?" asked Reginald.

"Yes, it is," said Yvette, casting her eyes down again.

"It's Richard who's made the house what it is today," continued Reginald. "It's been empty since Thomas's time. I believe no one wanted to take it on."

Yvette lifted her head, suddenly interested. "Oh, I didn't know that."

Richard was not happy with the way the conversation was going.

"Yes," continued Reginald. "Well, you know how superstitious people can be. I believe all sorts of rumours began after his death – the place being haunted by his restless spirit – you know the type of thing."

Yvette looked across at Richard. He looked disappointed, and was getting tired of the subject.

"Rumours like that can bother some people. But not you, eh, Richard?" smiled Reginald, as he looked across at him.

Richard sighed resignedly. "No, not me. I don't believe in that sort of thing."

Yvette looked at him. "I think there are some things even you can't explain."

Barbara and Reginald looked across at each other, sensing the atmosphere. Barbara tried to change the subject. She smiled at Yvette. "Have you got your wedding dress yet, my dear?"

Yvette brightened a little. "No, not yet, but it's all in hand. I'm going for a fitting next week."

Richard was pleased with the change of conversation. "Did you know my prospective wife has designed her own dress?"

"Really?" said Barbara. "Well, how charming. I can't wait to see it." She looked at Richard. "Are you going with her to the fitting, Richard?"

"No," smiled Richard. "Apparently it's bad luck for the groom to see the bride's dress before the wedding."

"Quite right too," smiled Barbara.

"Also, I've got to work that day, but I'll have Benson drive her into town."

"Oh, that seems a shame," said Barbara. Then to Yvette:

"What day are you going, my dear?"

"Next Wednesday," replied Yvette.

Barbara looked at Reginald. "Have I got anything on for next Wednesday, Regi?"

"Not that I know of," replied Reginald. "I'm going to Lord Maybury's, of course."

"How could I forget?" said Barbara.

"Got a fine chestnut mare for sale," continued Reginald. "16.2, three quarters thoroughbred, middleweight hunter. Just what I'm looking for."

"Good Lord," said Richard, "not another horse?"

"That's what I said," interjected Barbara. "But you know what he's like, Richard. Anyway, that needn't affect me." She turned to Yvette. "If you like, Yvette, I could come with you."

"I would like that very much," smiled Yvette. "As long as you're not spoiling your own arrangements?"

Reginald smiled at Yvette. "If I know Barbara, and I should by now," he glanced at Barbara, "she'll much prefer a day out with you than coming to Lord Maybury's with me." He leaned towards Yvette, and lowered his voice in mock confidentiality. "And to be honest, I'd prefer her to go with you too, because if she does come with me, she'll only try and talk me out of buying the mare." He leaned back in his chair, laughing.

Yvette began to laugh as well. Richard smiled across at her, happy her mood had changed. Then he looked at Barbara. She was smiling at Reginald, her love for him apparent.

"He's right, as well," said Barbara turning to Yvette. "I'd be much better going with you, Yvette. I could pick you up say, 11am, if that's suitable, and we could have lunch out, make a day of it."

Yvette was pleased with the prospect. She liked the Applebys very much, and could understand why Richard felt so close to them. They were quite a bit older than him, but that didn't get in the way of their deep friendship.

"Yes," agreed Yvette. "I would like that very much."

"Well, then that's settled," said Barbara.

They continued with their meal. Richard looked across at Yvette and winked at her. She smiled back, feeling happier now, and beginning to enjoy her evening.

Richard looked at Barbara and Reginald. "Actually, we want to ask you a favour."

"Oh?" said Barbara.

"As Yvette has no family, and Regi is going to be my best man," he looked at Barbara, "would you consider giving her away?"

Barbara was deeply moved, and very pleased. She looked at Yvette. "Oh, my dear, what an honour. Of course I will."

Yvette smiled at Barbara appreciatively. "That's so very kind of you, thank you. It will mean a lot to us both."

"Not at all, my dear, you've made me very happy." She turned to Reginald. "Oh, Regi, isn't that wonderful?"

"I think it's a splendid idea." He looked across to Richard and Yvette. "You're both very special to us, you know."

"I've got an idea," said Barbara. "Yvette could stay at Flaxted Hall on the eve of the wedding."

Yvette looked a little uncertain.

Barbara continued. "And be driven to the church from there in the morning. That way you won't see each other on the day, until you're both in the church. What d'you think?"

Yvette looked across at Richard. She wasn't sure about the idea. "I hadn't really thought about it. I could leave the manor beforehand, anyway, without seeing Richard. It's a very kind offer, but I think you're doing enough already."

"You'd be very welcome." Barbara turned to Reginald. "Wouldn't she, Regi?"

He smiled kindly at Yvette. "Of course. It would be a pleasure."

Barbara continued. "I know you are superstitious about Richard seeing the dress before the wedding."

"I think that's swung it, Barbara," smiled Richard. "We certainly don't want any bad luck, do we, darling?"

Yvette became a little solemn. "No, we don't," she answered.

"Well, then that's settled," said Barbara. "You'll be staying with us on the eve of your wedding."

Yvette smiled, but she was not entirely happy with the idea.

Later that night, they were all in the hallway, chatting. Maurice was helping the Applebys with their coats, then he went to the door and waited, in readiness for their departure.

"Well, it's been simply splendid, hasn't it, Regi?" said Barbera, as she put on her gloves.

"It certainly has, old girl," replied Reginald.

"It's been a pleasure having you both here. We must do it again some time," said Richard.

"Oh, you must come to us next time," said Barbara, then she went over to Yvette and kissed her on the cheek. "Goodbye, my dear. I'll see you on Wednesday morning."

"Yes," said Yvette. "I'm looking forward to it already."

Barbara gave Richard a peck on the cheek. "'Bye, Richard. Now you both take care of yourselves, and each other," she smiled.

"We will," replied Richard, shaking hands with Reginald. "'Bye, Regi. I hope all goes well with the horse."

"It will, old boy, it will."

Richard smiled across at Barbara. She shook her head resignedly. Then Reginald took Yvette's hand.

"Goodbye, Yvette. Have a good day on Wednesday." Then he lowered his voice. "And don't let Barbara take command," he joked. "She will if she can. I should know." They all walked to the door. "Thank you again," said Reginald, "for a splendid evening." They all walked outside, Reginald putting his hat on. "Brrr, it's cold, isn't it?"

The Applebys walked down the steps to their car. Reginald held the door open for Barbara, but before she got in, she turned and put her hand up in a wave to Richard and Yvette. They waved back.

"Goodnight," said Reginald. "And thank you again for this evening." He got in the car, the engine started, and the car moved away down the drive.

## THE PORTRAIT

Richard rubbed his hands together and Yvette shivered. "Regi's right," said Richard, "it is cold. Let's get inside." He put his arm around her as they walked into the hall, then Maurice closed the door. "We shan't be needing you any more tonight, Maurice, but thank you, and Mrs Worth for a splendid meal, and all your hard work."

"Not at all, sir, thank you. Goodnight." He walked away.

Richard took Yvette's arm. "It all went rather well, don't you think? Fancy a nightcap?" he asked.

But Yvette stopped by the stairs. "Would you mind, Richard, if I went straight to bed? I'm so tired."

Richard was surprised, and disappointed. "Of course not. Are you feeling all right?"

"Yes," smiled Yvette, not wanting to spoil his evening. "Just tired, that's all."

"Only, you seemed a little down earlier on."

"Yes, I'm sorry about that. I thought I was getting another headache, but it didn't come to anything," she lied. "I'm sorry if I appeared rude."

"That's all right," said Richard. "As long as you're all right."

"Yes, I am. I've enjoyed this evening."

"Well, you have a good sleep," said Richard, taking hold of her hand. "I'm so glad you had a nice time tonight." He still looked worried as he stroked her cheek. "If there is something wrong, you would tell me, wouldn't you? I only want you to be happy."

"Of course I would," she said. She looked at him a moment, then put her arms around him, and kissed him passionately. Then she looked into his eyes and said, "I do love you, Richard."

"And I love you, darling, and always will." He embraced her, then all went quiet and a voice said:

*"I love you, Catherine. I love you. Promise me we'll never part, for I could not live without you."*

Yvette pulled back suddenly and looked at Richard. "What did you say?" she asked.

"Nothing," replied Richard. Then he noticed she had gone ashen. "Yvette, what's wrong? You've gone very pale."

Yvette pulled herself together. "I'm all right, but I must go to bed," she smiled. "A good night's sleep will do me the world of good." She gave him a quick kiss on the cheek. "Goodnight," she said, then turned and began to walk up the stairs.

Richard watched her. "Goodnight. Sleep well," he said.

Once in her bedroom she closed the door, went over to the dressing table and took a couple of aspirin. She lay down on her bed fully clothed, and put her hand to her head. As she lay there, she remembered where she'd heard those words before: in the summerhouse.

# Fourteen

The next morning, outside the church, it was gloomy and very misty. The congregation were coming out after the service, and, the vicar, was shaking hands with people as they left. When he got to Yvette and Richard he said, "Nice to see you again. Won't be long now until the big day."

"No," smiled Richard. "By the way, where's Dorothy today?"

"Oh, she has a cold. Quite bad, as a matter of fact. I said it would be best for her to stay at home."

"That's a shame," said Yvette.

"Yes," said Richard. "Give her our regards and say we hope she's feeling better soon."

"I will," said David.

They turned to leave, then suddenly David remembered something. "Oh, Richard, if you're not in too much of a hurry, could I have a quick word with you?"

Richard and Yvette stood and waited whilst David shook hands with the remaining congregation, some of whom nodded and smiled as they walked past them. Then David turned to Richard. "It's that book you loaned me – I keep meaning to give it back to you. I brought it with me today, in the hope of seeing you. It's in the vestry. I'll just go and fetch it." As he walked back into the church, Richard called out:

"I'll come with you." He turned to Yvette. "Coming, darling?"

"No, I'll wait here, if you don't mind," she answered.

"As you like," he said, and followed David into the church.

Yvette looked around the churchyard. There were large trees dotted about, looking eerie in the mist. Rooks were flying overhead, calling to each other. She began to walk down one of the paths, following it around to the other side of the churchyard. Eventually she approached an area of very old gravestones, some upright, others flat. The grass was overgrown in this section. She stopped at intervals to read the inscriptions (those that were readable); others had succumbed to the weather, and over the years were almost worn away. Suddenly, she saw a large gravestone in the corner of the churchyard, near a tall oak tree. The grass had been trimmed around it, and it stood out from the rest, by its neatness. Curious, she walked over to it, then as she approached she began to feel uneasy. She knew what she was going to find, and she was right. It was the grave of Thomas and his parents. She read the inscription:

*In memory of Sir Ronald Courtney of Shearwater*
*Born 8 July 1763. Departed this life 9 August 1822*
*And his beloved wife Elizabeth*
*Born 27 FEBRUARY 1768. Departed this life*
*11 March 1825*
*And of their son Thomas Courtney*
*Born 6 January 1800. Departed this life*
*27 January 1829*
*May they rest in peace.*

## THE PORTRAIT

Just then, a breeze caught the branches of the tree. They creaked, and leaves came fluttering down. The crows cawed noisily overhead, then all was calm again. Yvette bent down slowly, and moved the leaves away with her hand. After a moment she stood up; she felt as though someone was watching her. Hesitantly she turned and looked over towards the side of the church. She knew who she would see, and there he was, through the mist, the same man as before, looking at her. She averted her gaze to look at the church porch, hoping to see Richard. She was relieved to see them both coming out of the door. She looked again to where the man had been standing, but he was gone. She walked quickly over to Richard. "Oh, Richard, you're here."

He was surprised by her manner. "Everything all right, darling?"

"Yes. I thought I'd wait inside the church – I felt a bit cold – but you're here now."

"Yes," said David, "it's a bit damp today, isn't it? Autumn is well on its way."

"Right," agreed Richard. "Anyway, thanks for the book. I'd forgotten all about it, to be honest."

"My fault for keeping it so long," replied David. "Well, see you both next week, hopefully."

"We'll be here," answered Richard. "'Bye."

"Goodbye," said David, as the pair made their way towards the gate.

Yvette was glancing around the churchyard as they walked, then her gaze fell upon the gravestone where she'd been standing minutes before. Suddenly, she realised Richard was looking at her. She smiled at him. As she passed through the gate, Richard glanced over to where Yvette had been looking, but there was no one there. They walked to the car. Richard held the door open for Yvette, then walked around to the other side and got in himself. After a moment the engine started, and they drove away. Inside the churchyard, standing by the gravestone, was the man, watching as they disappeared into the mist.

# Fifteen

That night, Yvette was in her negligee, sitting at the dressing table, brushing her hair. Then she heard soft footsteps passing her room. She sat still and listened. She was curious and got up and walked over to the door. After a moment she heard a door open and shut. She waited a few seconds then went out into the corridor. It was in darkness, but with the light from her room she could see no one was there. She walked towards the stairs and looked down over the banister. Again, the hallway was empty. As she walked back to her room, she noticed a faint glimmer of light coming from under the door at the end of the corridor. Her heart began to beat a little faster. She was apprehensive, but her curiosity got the better of her, and she walked towards the door. She put her ear against it and thought she heard someone moving very quietly inside. She tried the doorknob, but the door was locked. Then she looked down and saw there was no longer any light coming from within, as though it had suddenly been switched off. She stood a moment, perplexed, but then her fear overcame her and she walked (almost ran) back to her bedroom. She shut the door, and stood for a moment to compose herself.

The next morning, from outside the manor, a bright sun was shining, and Richard's car was parked outside. They were both at breakfast in the dining room. "It looks as if it's going to be another fine day," said Richard, spreading marmalade on a piece of toast. "I wish I didn't have to go into the office."

"Me too," answered Yvette ruefully.

"You really will have to find a hobby after the wedding, darling, or you're going to be very bored whilst I'm at work."

"Yes, I know," she replied. As they continued their breakfast, Yvette decided to broach the subject of the room at the end of the corridor, but pretended only a mild interest. "Richard," she began.

"Yes, darling?"

"Remember I was asking you the other day about that room at the end of the corridor?"

"Yes," he replied, uneasily.

She smiled at him. "Well, I was just wondering, could I have a look inside? Just to see what it's like."

Richard patted his mouth with his napkin, and said, evasively, "I told you, darling, it's just a room where I keep old documents. It would be of no interest to you. And anyway, I'm not sure where the key is at the moment."

Yvette was unconvinced, as he continued:

"Tell you what, as soon as I find it, I'll show you.
I can't say fairer than that, now can I?"

"No, I suppose not," said Yvette, crestfallen.

"By the way," said Richard, glad to change the subject, "Barbara phoned to say she'll pick you up at 10am rather than 11am on Wednesday. If there's a problem, just give her a call."

"No, that'll be all right," answered Yvette, still wondering why Richard wouldn't let her see the room.

# THE PORTRAIT

He got up from the table. "I must get going," he said, giving her a kiss on the cheek. "I shouldn't be too long today."

Yvette stayed in her seat. "All right."

He left, and a few minutes later she heard the engine start up, and the car drive away. It was going to be another long day, and her mind was in turmoil over the strange events that had occurred since she'd arrived at the manor. Richard was hiding something from her, she was certain. But what?

Wednesday morning came – a bright, sunny, autumnal day. In the sitting room Yvette was flipping through a magazine, waiting for Barbara. Richard was still at home, standing looking out of the window. He was on edge because Barbara was a little late. Yvette wondered why it should bother him. Usually by now he would have started out for the office.

He looked at his watch. "10.05," he said. "I hope she isn't going to be too much longer."

Yvette was surprised at his agitation. "Don't worry, Richard, she'll be here. Anyway, you've usually started out for the office by now."

"What? Oh, I don't need to be in until a bit later, and I wanted to say hello to Barbara, that's all," he lied.

Just then they heard someone at the front door. Moments later, Maurice showed Barbara into the room.

"Good morning to you both, sorry I'm a bit late."

Yvette got up and walked over to her. They gave each other a peck on the cheek.

"That's all right," said Yvette, looking across at Richard. "You're not late at all. Would you like a coffee before we leave?"

Richard almost shouted, "No!"

Yvette looked at him, surprised at his abrupt manner.

He was embarrassed. "Sorry, I didn't mean to be rude, but I'm sure you just want to be on your way, don't you Barbara?"

Barbara smiled. "Yes, we'd best be going. We've a beautiful day for it, anyway."

"I'll just get my coat and handbag," said Yvette.

"Really, darling, you should have brought them down with you," said Richard.

Yvette wondered why he seemed annoyed. "I won't be long." She looked at Barbara and smiled. "Honestly, Barbara, you'd think he was trying to get rid of me."

Barbara gave a weak smile.

In her bedroom, her coat, handbag and gloves were lying on the bed. She picked them up, but just as she was leaving the room, she heard a bumping sound coming from the room at the end of the corridor. She stopped a moment, wondering if she should try the door again, but Richard shouted from the hallway:

"Come on, darling, what's keeping you?"

She turned and walked downstairs.

Richard was looking anxiously at her. "Ah, at last," he said.

Yvette was putting on her gloves and smiled. "Sorry to keep you, Barbara."

"That's all right, my dear," she said kindly. "You don't need to hurry on my account."

Richard gave Barbara a stern look.

"Well," she continued, "if you've got everything, we'd best be on our way."

Richard opened the door for them. "Take your time, there's no need to rush back." He walked down the steps with them to the car. Barbara went to the driver's side, whilst Richard opened the passenger door for Yvette. He gave her a quick kiss. "Have a good day, both of you."

"We will," said Barbara.

Yvette settled into her seat and Richard closed the door.

"'Bye," he said.

"'Bye, Richard," they both answered. Then the engine started and the car moved away down the drive. Richard smiled as they went, and put his hand up in a wave. Then he ran up the steps, into the hall and closed the door. He leaned against it with a sigh of relief. Then he walked up the stairs, and made his way to the room at the end of the corridor. When he reached the door he knocked lightly. He heard footsteps crossing the floor, the key turned in the lock, the door opened and a shaft of light appeared from within. He walked inside.

Barbara and Yvette were travelling along. Yvette looked troubled. There were questions she wanted answers to, but could not ask Richard. Could she ask Barbara? Maybe she would know.

"You're very quiet, my dear. Is everything all right?" asked Barbara.

Yvette was suddenly aware. "Oh yes, I was just thinking, that's all." They continued on, then suddenly Yvette decided to confide in her. "Barbara."

"Yes, my dear?"

"Did you think Richard was a little anxious for us to be away from the house just now? He was rather brusque, almost to the point of being rude. I've never seen him like that before."

"I just think he's got a lot on his mind at present. What with his business, and the wedding, not to mention the book he's writing."

Yvette was not really convinced, but she said, "Yes, I suppose so." After a moment she continued. "I was looking around the churchyard on Sunday. Richard had some business with the vicar, so I went for a walk." She paused for a moment, then continued. "I found Thomas Courtney's grave, and that of his parents." She looked at Barbara. "It's been very well kept. I wondered how, when most of the other stones in that area are almost worn away, and overgrown."

"Yes," said Barbara. "Richard has an arrangement with his gardener. After he moved to the manor he was very taken with the history of the place and decided to have the grave looked after."

"Oh, I see," said Yvette.

"Yes, it's a family grave," continued Barbara, "and was almost completely obscured by ivy, brambles and so forth. The inscription was nearly illegible too, but now it's almost back to its original state. But for Catherine being killed in France, she would've been buried there as well."

"It was a terrible tragedy, wasn't it?" said Yvette.

"Dreadful," replied Barbara.

"Apparently, they'd been arguing just before, so Richard told me."

"Yes, I believe so," answered Barbara.

"It must be heartbreaking to part on an argument," continued Yvette. "To not have the chance to put things right."

## THE PORTRAIT

"It must be, especially for the one left behind. Maybe she was riding recklessly, or been thrown. We'll never really know." Barbara sensed Yvette's sadness so she grasped her hand to comfort her. "Come on, my dear, cheer up. It should be a happy day. You're on your way to your dress fitting, you've got the wedding to look forward to, and your life with Richard in a most beautiful home."

"Yes, I know," smiled Yvette, starting to feel better.

"Where are you going for your honeymoon?" asked Barbara.

"I don't know," answered Yvette. "Richard has made the arrangements, but he hasn't told me. He wants it to be a surprise."

"Oh, how romantic," said Barbara.

"Yes, I suppose so," replied Yvette, uncertainly. Suddenly she asked, "Do you have any children, Barbara?"

"No," she replied. "Oh, we wanted them, but it just never happened."

Yvette felt embarrassed. "Oh, I'm sorry. I didn't mean to pry."

"Not at all, my dear. It doesn't bother us anymore. It used to, but not now. I think not having children has brought us closer together."

Yvette looked across at Barbara and smiled. "Yes, I can see that. You both look so very happy."

Barbara glanced at Yvette. "And you and Richard will be happy too, my dear."

Yvette smiled at her, then turned her head to look out of the window. But her smile faded, as though she had some doubts. She had wanted to ask about the room at the end of the corridor, but thought she'd asked enough questions for one day. Anyway, Barbara may know nothing about it.

They reached the small town of Lindery. It was too early for lunch, so they went to a small café and ordered coffee. Yvette began to enjoy herself. She was excited at the prospect of seeing her dress, and wondered if her design had been followed correctly. They chatted easily to one another, and in no time at all it was 11.30.

"What time is your fitting did you say?" asked Barbara.

"1.30," replied Yvette.

"We'll have some lunch then before that. I know a little place just down the street. Their menu is a bit limited, and it takes a while to get your meal, but everything is all fresh, and is cooked whilst you wait, so it's worth it. And anyway, we've got plenty of time. We can perhaps do a bit of window shopping beforehand? Or is there anything else you would like to get whilst we're here?"

"Nothing I can think of," replied Yvette. "Do you need anything?"

"No," replied Barbara. "It's just nice to be out on such an exciting occasion. I can't wait to see your dress."

"Me too," said Yvette excitedly.

"One thing about Mrs Gilroy: she's a good dressmaker," said Barbara. "Most people around these parts go to her. She'll not let you down."

"That's good to hear," said Yvette. "I thought I'd asked too much of her, considering the time limit."

"She's very professional, and her assistants are just as good. I'm sure you'll be pleased."

They walked up and down the street, gazing in various windows, and soon it was time for lunch.

THE PORTRAIT

They went to the restaurant Barbara had suggested. It was quite small, but very clean. All the tables were covered with immaculate white tablecloths, the cutlery shone, and in the centre of each table was a small vase of carnations. They had an enjoyable meal and, before they knew it, it was time to make their way to the dressmaker's. Barbara insisted on paying for the meal, and would hear no argument. After a trip to the powder room, they came out of the restaurant, into the sunshine, and made their way to the dressmaker's.

They got there about 10 minutes early, but Mrs Gilroy was pleased to see them, and said she was ready to commence the fitting. They were asked to take a seat whilst Mrs Gilroy and one of her assistants fetched the dress. Yvette's heart was beating fast with the excitement of it all. She also felt a bit nervous, wondering what it would be like. She didn't have long to wait before the dress, protected by a large zipped white bag, was brought through.

"If you come with me, Miss Moreau, I'll take you to the fitting room." As they walked through, Barbara remained seated, and picked up a fashion magazine. In the fitting room, Yvette began to remove her outer clothing, with the help of the assistant. The dress was removed from the bag, and there it was: a white satin dress, gathered at the waist with lace covering the bodice, and lace sleeves to the wrist. Yvette felt a flush of excitement as they helped her put it on. Then it was fastened at the back. There was a full-length mirror in the fitting room, and Yvette looked at her reflection, turning this way and that. It was beautiful, and her design had been copied exactly. "It's stunning," said Yvette, becoming emotional. "Could I show Mrs Appleby?"

"Yes, of course," said Mrs Gilroy. "But I will need to make one or two small alterations. Apart from that, I think we're there."

Yvette smiled as she went into the main shop. Barbara was sitting, looking through the magazine. She looked up as Yvette came into the room. "Oh, my dear, how beautiful you look," she said emotionally.

Yvette was pleased. "You like it?"

"Very much," replied Barbara.

"It is from Miss Moreau's own design," said Mrs Gilroy.

"Yes, I know," said Barbara, as she looked on in admiration.

Yvette turned to Mrs Gilroy. "You've made it beautifully. I'm so very pleased."

"Thank you," she said, and went back into the room from where she had brought the dress, and returned with the veil. It was long and made of lace which trailed down at the back of the dress, on to the train. It was clipped into place, so Yvette could see the full effect.

"What flowers are you going to have?" asked Barbara.

"Red roses," replied Yvette.

"Oh, what a beautiful choice."

"Yes, stunning," agreed Mrs Gilroy.

The shop also had a full-length mirror, and Yvette walked over to it, and turned to view the dress from the side and the back. She smiled with delight as she turned to face the mirror, but suddenly, she could no longer hear the comments from the others in the room. There was complete silence, and as she stared at her reflection, her face turned to horror. Instead of the dress she was wearing, another dress was reflected back at her – beautiful, but not Yvette's dress. It was white satin, but fuller in the skirt, and there were small, silk white roses along the neckline, and here and there on the veil, which was covering the face. The figure was holding a bouquet of red roses. As Yvette stood in disbelief, the reflection raised one hand to lift the veil. Before she had fully revealed her face, Yvette was suddenly aware Barbara had taken her arm and was saying:

"Yvette, Yvette? Are you all right?"

Yvette slowly turned to her, as the others looked on, concerned.

"Come and sit down," said Mrs Gilroy. "Would you like a glass of water?"

After a few moments, Yvette gathered her thoughts, and spoke slowly and quietly. "I'm all right, I'm all right. I just felt a bit faint."

The assistant returned with a glass of water and Yvette sipped it. Her face had been ashen, but now some colour was returning.

Barbara looked concerned. "Do you need a doctor?" she asked.

"No," answered Yvette. "No, I shall be all right in a minute. I think it's all the excitement," she lied. She knew she couldn't mention what she had seen for people would think her mad.

"When you're ready, and only if you feel well enough, we can go back to the fitting room and I'll make those final adjustments. It won't take me long," said Mrs Gilroy.

After a few moments, Yvette stood up, handing the glass back to the assistant with thanks. She walked a little unsteadily, but before she went into the fitting room she glanced at the mirror. Now her own reflection looked back at her. She was relieved, but what had happened had frightened and upset her. She had been having such a lovely day until then. She decided she must put it behind her and try to carry on as normal, otherwise it would worry Barbara and spoil her day as well. She entered the fitting room with Mrs Gilroy and her assistant. They set about tweaking the dress, putting in pins here and there. Mrs Gilroy was right, it didn't take long. Yvette was glad of that. She hadn't really felt like it. But soon she was back in her normal clothes, and standing in the shop with Barbara. "Thank you so much, Mrs Gilroy," said Yvette. "You've worked wonders, and in such a short time as well."

"Not at all," she replied. "I'm pleased you are happy with it."

"Very much," said Yvette. Then after a moment she said, "I'm sorry about before. I don't know what came over me."

"It's so warm today, isn't it? Quite airless. But as long as you're all right now, that's the main thing," said Mrs Gilroy, kindly.

"Yes," replied Yvette, but with not much conviction. "I'm all right now."

"Come along, my dear," said Barbara. Then to Mrs Gilroy:

"Thank you so much. I told Yvette you wouldn't let her down."

"I can arrange to have the dress delivered next week," Mrs Gilroy said to Yvette. "It will save you having to come into the town."

"Yes," replied Yvette, "that would be lovely, thank you."
"Not at all," smiled Mrs Gilroy.
They said their goodbyes, and moments later Yvette and Barbara were outside the shop. They walked along in silence for a moment, then Yvette said:

"Thank you for coming with me today, Barbara. It was so nice to have someone else's opinion. It's been a lovely day." She tried not to think about what had happened. "But now it's time for home, don't you think?"

Barbara looked at her watch, and was a little uneasy. "Do you fancy some tea and cake, before we start out? We could go to the teashop on Acacia Street. It's just around the corner. It's very nice."

Yvette smiled. "Yes, I could do with a cup of tea, but perhaps no cake for me."

"As you like," said Barbara.

Minutes later they entered the teashop. The tables were set with white lacy tablecloths. There was a stand of cakes on doilies in a corner; shiny teapots, water and milk jugs on a trolley near the counter. On the tables were beautifully patterned china cups and saucers, and a small vase of tiny pink roses in the centre. A waitress, in a black dress and white apron, with a lacy cap on her head, came over and showed them to a table, then stood with pad and pencil in hand, awaiting their order.

"Two English teas, please," ordered Barbara. "And will you bring the cake stand too?"

"Of course, madam," said the waitress, and walked away.

"I really don't want a cake, Barbara. I don't feel hungry."

"Have a little something, my dear, even if you can't eat it all."

Yvette didn't want to appear miserable and spoil the day for Barbara, so she agreed. "All right," she smiled, "just a small one, perhaps."

Barbara looked pleased. "Splendid," she said.

Just then the tea arrived, and as the waitress put down the teapots, water and milk jugs, another waitress came over with the cake stand.

Barbara cast her eyes over the cakes, then said, "A piece of gateau, please."

"Very good, madam," said the waitress as she took a plate and serving tongs, lifted the cake skilfully onto the plate, and placed it on the table before Barbara.

"Thank you," she said. "And for you, my dear? What would you like?"

Yvette glanced over the cake stand and picked out one of the smaller cakes. "A chocolate eclair, please," she said.

Again the waitress picked up the cake, put it on a plate and placed it before Yvette.

"Thank you," smiled Yvette.

The waitresses moved away, and after a few moments Barbara smiled and asked, "Shall I be mother?"

"Oh, yes please, if you don't mind," replied Yvette.

Barbara poured the teas, and they helped themselves to milk and sugar, then Barbera started on her gateau. Yvette looked at her cake. It was nice and fresh, the chocolate glistening on the pastry and the cream oozing out along the length of it. With an effort she took up her cake fork and picked up a small piece. It took a while for her to chew and then swallow it. Although it was a beautiful cake, it felt like cardboard in her mouth as she made an effort to eat it.

Barbara looked across at her. "Is it nice?" she asked.

"Yes," said Yvette, "it's lovely." And just to please Barbara, she lifted another piece to her mouth, and chewed slowly.

"Look, my dear, don't eat it if you don't want it. I did railroad you into it, after you said you weren't hungry, so it's my fault."

"No really, it's nice. Although I don't think I can eat all of it."

"Then don't," smiled Barbara.

Yvette put down the cake fork with some relief, then took a sip of her tea.

After a few moments, Barbara asked kindly, "Don't think I'm prying, my dear, but there's nothing wrong is there?"

"What d'you mean?" asked Yvette.

"Well, it's just that you seem a little on edge. If there is something, you can tell me. If it will help. It'll go no further, I promise."

Yvette looked across at Barbara's kind face. She desperately wanted to confide in someone about what had been happening, then on impulse she decided to tell her. "Oh, Barbara—"

That's as far as she got, as the waitress came to the table and asked if everything was all right for them, and did they want anything else.

"No, we're fine, thank you," said Barbara, and the waitress walked away. Barbara looked across at Yvette. "Go on, my dear, you were about to say?"

But the moment had passed.

"Oh, it's nothing," she smiled weakly. "I've just been feeling a bit low at times, that's all. I know I've got lots to look forward to, but Richard's been so busy, I've had a lot of time on my hands." She took another sip of her tea.

Barbara studied her a moment. She was not convinced that was what Yvette had meant to tell her. After a moment she said, "You must find an interest, a hobby of some kind. If you don't, you'll go out of your mind. But you need never be lonely, you know. You're always welcome to visit us. We'd be happy to see you, any time."

Yvette was touched by her sincerity. "Thank you, Barbara, that's very kind. I hope after the wedding we'll be entertaining more. I'd enjoy that."

Barbara patted her lips with her napkin. "Richard's never been one for parties and such, but once you're married, who knows? You must put your foot down," smiled Barbara.

Yvette smiled back.

"Are you sure there's nothing else you want to tell me?" continued Barbara.

"No, nothing," replied Yvette. Then, after a moment: "I'll just pay the waitress, then we can go."

"No, you don't," said Barbara sternly. "It was my idea to come here, and if I want to treat you, I will do," she smiled, as she got up from the table.

"But you paid for lunch," Yvette pointed out.

"That doesn't matter," said Barbara as she walked to the counter.

Yvette realised there was no point arguing. She got up from the table and put on her coat. Moments later Barbara was back, she did the same and, making sure they had everything, left the teashop.

THE PORTRAIT

It was still sunny, but humid, as they walked along chatting. Soon they were at the car. Barbara rooted in her bag for the car keys. "Ah, here they are," she said, unlocking the doors. "I'm taking this off." Barbara removed her coat, and put it on the back seat.

"Yes, you're right to," said Yvette, doing the same.

"It's so warm, I shouldn't be at all surprised if we have a storm later," said Barbara.

"Yes, perhaps. But I've had a lovely day. Thank you for coming. It made it so much nicer than Benson bringing me. He's very nice, but I wanted somebody who could give me some advice, and reassurance that the dress was all right."

"All right?" said Barbara. "It's more than all right – it's beautiful. And anyway, if you asked Benson about something bridal, he'd probably think you wanted some tack for the horses."

Yvette laughed as they continued on their journey.

"Actually," said Barbara, "I was thinking of going a different way back, if that's all right with you? It'll give you a chance to see more of the countryside, and I think you'll enjoy it."

"All right," answered Yvette. "Whatever you wish."

"It'll add about half an hour to our journey, but it's very pleasant."

"Though perhaps we should go straight back, if you think there's as storm brewing?" said Yvette.

"Oh, it's still quite fine, and there's no hurry, is there? As long as you're feeling all right, that is."

"Yes, I'm fine, thank you." Yvette began wondering why Barbara wanted to take a longer route. Surely she was tired after such a long day. But she said nothing.

111

They drove on in silence for a few minutes, then Barbara said, "By the way, Regi and I wondered if you and Richard would like to come to dinner on the eve of the wedding. You're coming to stay over anyway, but I thought we could make an evening of it. What d'you think?"

Yvette smiled. "Yes, that would be very nice. I'll ask Richard to give you a ring to confirm."

"Righto."

After a few moments Yvette said, "Do you think Reginald will have bought that horse?"

"I think it's a foregone conclusion, my dear. She'll be there when I get home, I'm sure of it." She glanced across at Yvette and smiled. "She's a beautiful animal. I've seen her out hunting, but I think she's a little green for Regi's needs. I don't know why he can't just settle for something a bit quieter. But he refuses to mellow, I'm afraid."

They continued on their way, chatting, and soon they were travelling up the driveway of Shearwater Manor.

"You will come in for tea?" asked Yvette.

"Oh, I won't, if you don't mind. I may as well get back and see if that blasted mare has arrived."

"Oh yes, of course," said Yvette. "Well, thank you once again for today."

"Don't mention it," replied Barbara. "We'll have to do it again sometime, after the wedding, when things have quietened down."

"I'd like that," smiled Yvette.

Barbara gave a quick glance at the house. She seemed uneasy. Yvette noticed this, and also glanced towards the house, wondering what Barbara had been looking at. Then Barbara leaned over and gave Yvette a quick peck on the cheek.

"Goodbye, my dear, take care. And remember what I said, you're welcome to come over any time."

Yvette smiled appreciatively. "Thank you, Barbara, you're very kind."

"Not at all, my dear, it'd be a pleasure."

As Yvette got out of the car, picking her coat off the back seat, Barbara suddenly remembered and said:

"Oh, and don't forget to ask Richard about the prenuptial dinner. Just let me know if it will be all right."

"Of course," replied Yvette. "Thanks again for today. 'Bye."

"Goodbye, my dear," and with that she drove away.

Yvette turned and looked at the house, feeling uneasy. Her smile faded as she walked towards the door. She opened it and walked into the hall. Maurice was coming out of the drawing room.

"Oh, Miss Moreau, you're back."

"Yes," replied Yvette.

"I trust you had a pleasant day?"

"Yes, thank you, Maurice. I don't suppose Mr Anderson is back yet?"

"Back, miss?"

"From the office?" continued Yvette.

"Oh yes, the office," he smiled. "Yes, miss, he's working in the study."

Yvette was a little surprised Richard was home already. Then she remembered his mood that morning. "Oh, I see. Well, I won't disturb him. I'll just go to my room and freshen up."

"Very good, miss," and he walked through the door leading to the kitchen.

Yvette walked slowly up the stairs and towards her bedroom. She glanced at the door at the end of the corridor, then walked into her room. She suddenly felt depressed. She threw her coat and handbag on the bed, then walked over to the dressing table and sat on the stool. Feeling tired, she put her elbows on the table and rested her head in her hands. Something was going on, and she was sure Maurice was in on it, maybe even Barbara. She must have it out with Richard. She could not bear him keeping secrets from her, that's not what a marriage should be. If it was something she couldn't accept, then she would have to return to France.

# Sixteen

As Yvette sat there, deep in thought, there was a knock at the door. "Come in," she said.

Richard walked in. He was smiling as he held out his arms and walked towards her. "Yvette, my darling."

She got up, pleasantly surprised at his welcoming manner; so different from that morning.

He kissed her. "Well, how was the dress?"

Yvette remembered what had happened at the dressmaker's. She smiled weakly. "Oh, the dress." She sat down again, picked up her brush and started to brush her hair. "It's beautiful. She's copied my design exactly."

"Splendid," said Richard. "Didn't Barbara want to come in for tea?"

"No. I asked her, but she wanted to get back." She looked at Richard's reflection in the mirror. "You're home early."

"Sorry?" asked Richard.

"From the office. I didn't expect you back so soon, especially as you didn't leave until later this morning."

"Ah, yes." He looked at her for a moment, then took her hand. "Come with me, I've got something to show you." Richard led a curious Yvette from the bedroom. Then he led her towards the door at the end of the corridor. Yvette looked nervous and her heart beat faster. At the door Richard took out a key from his pocket. He unlocked the door and slowly opened it, stepping away from the entrance as he did so. Bright daylight spilled out into the corridor. Richard smiled at Yvette. She looked at him perplexed. "Go on then," he smiled. "You've been wanting to see this room for some time, haven't you?"

Yvette walked slowly into the room, Richard following her. She glanced around. It was a very big room with a large window overlooking the gardens and parkland at the front, and a smaller window at the other end of the room which overlooked the walled garden at the back. Heavy, but beautiful curtains adorned both windows, which had been left slightly open, making the curtains move slightly in the breeze. There was also a fireplace. She took in the lavish furniture. A Persian rug covered most of the room, with a polished wooden floor surrounding it. There were paintings on the walls, mostly flowers, but also pretty country scenes. What shocked Yvette was the size of the bed. It was huge. It had a wooden headboard, which had been ornately carved, and on the bed, plush pillows and a beautiful satin quilt. It was as if she were in a dream. She walked slowly around the room, then she turned to Richard. She felt emotional; all this time believing he was keeping a secret from her. She smiled at him. This was the happiest time she'd had since she arrived at the manor. After a moment she spoke. "I don't know what to say. This is so beautiful."

"I'm glad you like it," said Richard. "Sorry it's taken so long to let you in on it, but I wanted it to be a surprise."

"But this is all new," she said.

"Very new," smiled Richard. "That night I was home very late, I'd been to London to sort it all out. Most of it was only delivered today. It's been quite a job."

"So that's why you wanted me away from the house this morning?"

"I was worried the delivery would come before you left. It would have spoiled the surprise. I'm sorry I was so brusque. I asked Barbara to keep you away for as long as possible."

"So Barbara was in on it as well. I wondered why she'd taken the longer route home," smiled Yvette. She looked around the room again, thrilled at what she was seeing.

"It was my room when I first came here," explained Richard, "but for some reason I couldn't settle in it. I think it was because it felt too large for one person, so I moved into the bedroom where I am now. I used this as a guest room. All the furniture in your room used to be in here."

Yvette noticed a dressing table by the front window. It had a new brush and comb set on it. She went over and picked them up.

"A little gift for you," said Richard. "I know you already have a set, but I saw these and thought you might like them."

"They're beautiful," said Yvette. She put them down and walked over to him. "You don't know what this means to me," she said. "I knew you were keeping something from me, but now it's all explained. I suppose Maurice was in on it too?"

"I couldn't have managed without him. Everybody has worked non-stop since you went out this morning."

Yvette suddenly thought of something. "Was it you, or Maurice, that was in here late on Sunday night? Only I thought I saw a light under the door."

"Well, it certainly wasn't me," said Richard. "Maybe it was Maurice, although I did tell him not to come into the room when you were upstairs."

"Well, it doesn't matter," said Yvette. "The door was locked anyway." She went over to the window and looked out over the lawns towards the parkland. After a moment she asked, "I expect this would've been Thomas and Catherine's room all those years ago." She turned to Richard.

"I imagine so," he replied. Then, a little disappointed, "That doesn't bother you, does it?"

"No, of course not," she lied. She walked over to him and put her arms around him. "It's beautiful, Richard. Thank you so much."

Richard smiled. "I'm so pleased you like it. It makes it all worthwhile." He kissed her, then said, "I love you, darling."

"And I love you," she replied.

In the distance there was a rumble of thunder. The sky became darker. Richard looked towards the window. "Looks like we're in for a storm. At least it'll clear the air." He took her hand and said, "Come on, let's have some tea."

They walked over to the door. Richard held it open for her. Before she left, she turned and looked into the room again. There was a flash of lightning and another rumble of thunder. Then she smiled weakly at Richard, and walked out of the room. He followed and closed, but did not lock, the door.

# Seventeen

That night, Yvette was in bed, lying on her side looking towards the window, which was closed due to the storm. The rain, even now, was battering against the panes. She had enjoyed her day for the most part, and now the mystery of the locked room was a mystery no longer. She felt a warm glow when she thought how Richard had worked so hard to make her happy. And she was happy. So why had she a niggling doubt in her mind? She turned over, closed her eyes and tried to sleep.

The next morning the storm was over. There was a low mist covering the gardens and parkland; the sun was trying its best to come through. In the stable yard, Benson was holding Richard's horse, Sultan, whilst the blacksmith tended to his shoes. The young stable lad, Joe, was mucking out, and there was a wheelbarrow of dirty straw outside the stable door. At the garage, Richard's car had been driven out and washed by Joe an hour earlier, and was gleaming.

In his study, Richard was on the telephone to Barbara, just finishing their conversation. "Well, thanks for ringing, Barbara. I was going to ring you later, to thank you for keeping Yvette away from the house yesterday. We'd not long finished when she arrived home, so it was perfect."

"Not at all. I'm so glad she's happy with the room."

"Yes, she really is," he said. "Anyway, we look forward to seeing you both next week," continued Richard. "'Bye for now." His smile faded as he put the receiver down. He walked out of the room just as Maurice was crossing the hall. "Oh, Maurice, have you seen Miss Moreau?"

"I believe she's in the drawing room, sir."

"Thank you. I'll be leaving for the office shortly. Would you bring my coat and briefcase please, and have the car sent round?"

"Very good, sir." Maurice walked upstairs.

Richard went to see Yvette in the drawing room. She was arranging flowers, and had almost finished, but she was just putting the finishing touches to them. She looked up as Richard walked in. "Aren't they beautiful, Richard? Benson brought them around to the kitchen this morning. Maurice was going to do them, but I offered. It gave me something to do."

"Well, you've done an excellent job," said Richard.

She picked up the vase and carried it over to a table by the window.

"I've just been speaking to Barbara on the telephone."

"Oh yes," Yvette answered. "I'm sorry, I forgot with all the excitement yesterday. She asked if we would like to come for dinner on the eve of the wedding."

"Yes, I know," said Richard. "I've confirmed it will be all right."

"I hope she wasn't offended by my forgetting to ask you."

"Of course not," said Richard. "Actually, she rang to ask how you were."

Yvette became uneasy. "Oh?"

"She said you were unwell yesterday at the dressmaker's. You never told me. Why?"

Yvette dismissed it. "It was nothing."

"Barbara was worried," replied Richard.

"She's making more of it than is necessary. I felt a little dizzy, that's all. It was all the excitement with the dress, and it was very warm in the shop."

Concerned, Richard put his hands on her shoulders, and looked searchingly into her eyes. "You're not sorry you came here, are you?"

Yvette was taken aback. "What? Of course not."

"She said you seemed troubled."

"It was nothing. She shouldn't have told you."

"She's concerned about you."

"She's very kind, but really, I'm all right." She smiled.

"And are you happy here?" he asked.

"Yes. I'm happy." She turned back to the flowers and started fiddling with them, her smile faded.

Just then there was a knock at the door, and Maurice came in. "Excuse me, sir, the car's ready for you."

"Right. Thank you, Maurice."

"Very good, sir," and he left the room.

"I'm sorry, darling, but I'll have to go."

Yvette took Richard's arm. "I'll come and see you off," she smiled.

They left the drawing room and walked over to the front door. Maurice helped him on with his coat, then handed him his hat and briefcase. He opened the door for them, and they walked outside, and stood at the top of the steps.

"I wanted to ask you something," said Yvette.

"Yes?" asked Richard.

"The book you're writing on Thomas and Catherine – how are you getting on with it? Is there anything ready yet that I can read?"

"Truthfully, darling, I've decided to put it aside for a while."

"Oh. Why?" she asked.

"I think I'm suffering from writers' block," he smiled, "what with everything that's going on at the moment. I'll give it another try after the wedding. Anyway, I must go." He kissed her then ran down the steps. "I'll see you later, darling. 'Bye." After a few moments he drove away.

Yvette watched the car until it was out of sight, then turned and walked back inside, closing the door behind her. She stopped a moment before deciding to take another look at what would be their bedroom. She walked upstairs, and towards the door. She knew she would have to stop this feeling of apprehension. Outside the door she stopped for a moment before opening it, and then walked slowly inside. She looked around her. The front window was open, and there was a lovely fresh feeling to the room. She walked over to the bed and sat down, facing the window. It was very pleasant. The birds were singing and woodpigeons cooed in the trees. It was so peaceful. The curtains moved slightly in the breeze.

Suddenly, a strong gust blew, making the curtains billow out into the room. Yvette closed her eyes softly, enjoying the sensation of it on her face, then the breeze died down again. She opened her eyes, got up and walked over to the window. She stared across the lawns and parkland beyond. Benson, with a wheelbarrow and gardening tools, was edging the lawns. After a moment her mind began to wander. She imagined how it must have been at Christmas in Thomas and Catherine's time, with snow covering the ground. *It would be late afternoon and the light would be fading, but the snow was keeping everything bright. The sky was clear; there would be a frost that night. A large red sun is going down in the distance, adding a pink hue to the snow, as a coach and four horses approaches the manor. Four people alight, a young couple and the parents of one of them, chatting excitedly, arriving for the Christmas festivities. They are carrying gifts, and two footmen come from the house to help them. The younger woman of the four guests looks up to the bedroom window, where Yvette now stands, and waves happily.* So real was the moment that Yvette raised her hand in reply.

Suddenly the scene outside changed to what it was before: the birds singing and Benson, a little further along now, trimming the lawns. Yvette stared pensively out of the window, then suddenly she heard a voice from behind say:

*"Catherine."*

Yvette was afraid to turn around, but turn around she must. There was no one there. She walked from the room and closed the door.

# Eighteen

Outside the church on Sunday, hymns could be heard being sung from within. Rooks were in the trees and flying around, making a noise with their cawing. Leaves blew over Thomas's grave. Inside the church, there were a lot of people standing and singing. Yvette and Richard were near the front. They were also singing, although Yvette was unfamiliar with the hymn. When it finished, she slowly lowered her hymnbook, then David, the vicar, asked them all to sit down. After a moment he picked up a piece of paper from the lectern and read: "I publish the banns of marriage between James Edward Smith, bachelor of this parish, and Sarah Jane Martin, spinster, also of this parish." A young couple across the aisle smiled at each other and giggled, a little embarrassed, as the congregation smiled and nodded their approval. "This is for the first time of asking," continued David. "Also between Richard Henry Anderson, bachelor of this parish, and Yvette Marie Moreau, spinster, also of this parish. This is for the third and final time of asking. Should any person know of any just cause or impediment why these persons should not be joined in holy wedlock, they are to declare it, or forever hold their peace."

Suddenly, the door at the back of the church blew open with a bang. The congregation, shocked by the suddenness of it, turned around to see what had happened, some of them murmuring to each other. A sidesman got up and closed the door, and the congregation turned back again in their seats. Yvette was troubled.

Outside the manor that night, it was late and the house was in darkness. There were large clouds scurrying over a three-quarter moon. The wind was in the trees, their branches waving and creaking. In the distance a fox barked. At the stable block the horses were restless, and Sultan, looking over his stable door, gave a shrill whinny, whilst the others, also looking out into the night, tossed their heads. There was a presence, but no one could be seen. After a short while, the horses settled down again, and all but Sultan turned their heads back into the stables.

In Yvette's bedroom, she was asleep, the room in darkness except for a little moonlight shining in through the slightly open window, the breeze gently moving the partially closed curtains. Yvette was dreaming; her eyelids flickered as she slept. She turned restlessly and continued to sleep. She was dreaming of the church, and the wedding. She could see herself walking up the aisle, towards the alter. She noticed the congregation turning to look at her, smiling as she passed them. Barbera walked beside her. Then she stood beside the groom and the vicar commenced the service. She felt in a trance, but she made the vows. Then it was the groom's turn. He too repeated the vows. A murmur of approval could be heard from the congregation as the vicar pronounced them husband and wife. Then they turned to each other, and Yvette lifted her veil, but looked on in disbelief. It was not Richard but Thomas Courtney smiling back at her. He took her hand and kissed it.

Yvette woke up suddenly and sat up in bed, breathing deeply. After a moment, she turned on the bedside lamp. She put her hand to her head which was aching. She got up and went to her dressing table and took out a couple of aspirin, taking them with a glass of water. After a moment she went over to the window and looked out. The garden below was dimly lit by the three-quarter moon, but there was enough light to see if anyone was there. The fox barked again, but now a little closer. She could see no one, then there was movement by the garden seat. She focused her gaze, but suddenly a cloud covered the moon and the light was gone. She walked back to her bed and lay down, putting her arm across her forehead. After a moment, a tear trickled down her face.

# Nineteen

Next morning the sky was overcast, but the wind had died down. Richard and Yvette came out of the front door, Yvette with her arm through his. He was dressed for the office and held his hat and briefcase. "It's going to be warm again," he said.

"Yes. I think I'll go for a walk this afternoon, if it brightens up," said Yvette.

"Well don't get caught out, there's a storm forecast for later."

Yvette smiled. "Oh, I shan't be going far."

Richard kissed her, and walked down the steps to the car. Yvette waved as he drove away, then turned and walked back inside. She was going to go to her room, but had just seen Mrs Parker, the cleaner, and her daughter Sarah, carrying fresh bed linen to the bedrooms. She knew they'd be a while, so she walked into the sitting room and sat on the settee. She picked up a magazine and flipped through it, though she wasn't really interested. She put it down and found her gaze focusing on the portrait. She got up, walked over to it and looked at Thomas's handsome features, just as they were in her dream last night. She turned away and walked over to the window and stood looking over the garden. In the distance Benson was mowing the lawns. She watched him for a while, then suddenly she could hear, ever so faintly, the sounds of voices – a man and a woman talking and laughing. It echoed around her, but Yvette was not afraid. In fact she felt quite calm. Then the door opened behind her, the voices stopped and she turned to see who had entered. It was Johnathan, Maurice's assistant, carrying logs for the fire.

"Sorry, miss," he said. "I didn't think anyone was in here."

"That's all right," said Yvette, kindly.

"Would you like me to light the fire, miss?"

"Oh, no thank you, I'll not be here for long."

Johnathan smiled a little sheepishly, and began to put the logs in the basket by the fire, then he left the room. Yvette stood for a moment wondering if the voices would come back, but she heard nothing further. She glanced again at the portrait, then left the room, closing the door behind her.

That afternoon the weather had improved. The sun had come out and it was warm. Yvette had lunched, and decided to go for a walk in the gardens. She felt light-hearted, and wondered why she should feel so elated. She wandered past the stables – she would not go there today – and kept walking until she came to the overgrown part of the gardens, which led to the summerhouse. She stopped a moment, in thought. The other day she had not wanted to go there again on her own, but she felt differently today. She continued on her way to the summerhouse. There it was, derelict, a place where happiness had once been; probably Thomas and Catherine's special place, where they would have spent afternoons together, surrounded by beautifully kept lawns and flowers. *Especially roses*, she thought. What a shame to see it like this. She hoped Richard would ask

Benson if he could do something with it, and with the tangled and overgrown gardens that surrounded it. It would be a lot of work; he would need some help.

She arrived at the summerhouse and stood for a moment looking through what had once been a doorway. It was just as before. What was she expecting? She walked inside. It was brighter today because of the sun shining through the gaping roof. She looked out of where a window had once been. She turned and looked at the stone seat, where the rose had lain the last time she was here, but there was no rose today. She felt relieved. Just then she heard a rumble of thunder in the distance. She decided to go back to the manor before the rain started.

It was very warm, almost airless; thin cloud now covered the sun. She walked slowly back, feeling tired. It was so warm, she hoped there would be a storm to clear the air. She thought she would go to her room and have a lie down before Richard got back. She walked across the hall, up the stairs, and into her bedroom. She closed the door and turned to face the room. She felt her heart give a jolt and begin to beat faster. There on her pillow was a red rose. She ran out of the room and downstairs. Maurice was on his way across the hall when she sped past him.

"Are you all right, miss?" he asked.

But Yvette did not answer. She ran into the sitting room. Richard was sitting in a chair, reading a newspaper. He looked up in surprise as she rushed into the room, then she stopped when she saw him.

"Oh, Richard, you're back."

"Yes, darling," he said, getting up from his chair. "Is something wrong?"

"No," she said breathlessly. "Nothing." She went over to him and hugged him tightly. She was near to tears.

"Something has upset you," he said, looking at her face.

"No, really, I'm all right now." She searched quickly for an explanation for her behaviour, then said lamely, "I saw a big spider in my room, on the bed. I have a fear of them, you know."

"Really? I didn't know that." He didn't make fun of her – he saw how upset she was. "Come and sit down," he said. "Maurice is bringing some tea. It'll make you feel better." They sat beside each other on the settee. "It's a pity I didn't see it when I was in there," said Richard. "I could have spared you the fright."

Yvette looked at him. "You were in my room?"

"Yes. I left something for you on your pillow."

Yvette smiled weakly. "You left a rose?"

"Yes. You know what a romantic I am," he smiled.

Just then, Maurice entered the room with the tea trolley. There were sandwiches, and cakes as well. He had brought a proper afternoon tea. "Will there be anything else, sir, miss?"

"Yes, Maurice. You're not afraid of spiders, are you?"

Maurice looked perplexed. "No, sir."

"Well, there's one in Miss Moreau's room, last seen on the bed." he smiled. "It's quite a large one apparently. Do you think you could catch it and put it outside? Miss Moreau has a fear of them."

"Certainly, sir, if I can find it."

"No," said Yvette. "No, it's all right. It went on the floor and ran out of the room as I opened the door," she lied.

"Oh, well in that case, that'll be all, thank you, Maurice."

"Very good, sir, miss." He left the room.

"Are you feeling better now?" asked Richard.

"Yes, much better thank you," she smiled. "I'll pour the tea."

That night, from the rose garden, the light from Yvette's window could be seen. She suddenly appeared at the window and closed it to keep out the rain, which was now torrential.

Later, in the dining room, Richard and Yvette were having their evening meal. The fire was lit, as the rain had cooled the air down, and the curtains were drawn against the night. Richard was eating his meal, unaware that Yvette was looking across at him, watching him. Then he looked up and saw her. He smiled. She smiled back then continued with her meal. A little later, after their meal, they were in the sitting room. Again the curtains were drawn and the fire was lit, giving a warm glow to the room. Various lamps were lit, and Richard and Yvette were sitting together on the settee. Richard had his arm around her, and she leant against him. They were both staring at the fire. The logs crackled as the flames licked them. Richard looked down and kissed the top of Yvette's head. Yvette inclined her face towards him and smiled, then turned her gaze on the portrait. The flames from the fire were flickering across Thomas's face. Yvette's smile faded. She looked into the fire again, and continued with her thoughts.

Outside in the rose garden, a flash of lightning lit up the two statuettes. In the summerhouse, the rain was pouring through the roof and broken windows. Another flash lit up the scene. There was someone there, but when the next flash came, they were gone.

Later that night, Yvette was in bed with her bedside lamp on, reading a book. The curtains were closed against the storm raging outside. On her bedside table was a candle and matches, ready, should the lights go out again. She wasn't really concentrating on her book – her thoughts kept milling around in her head – and when the bedside lamp began to flicker, she put the book down and turned off the lamp.

In the early hours of the morning, outside the manor the fury of the storm was over. Leaves and branches were strewn across the lawns and driveway; downspouts, overwhelmed by so much rain, were overflowing. In her bedroom Yvette was asleep, her right hand resting on her pillow. Then she woke suddenly. She could hear something. She sat up in bed, and listened. There was that sound again, like someone crying. It wasn't the wind, as Richard had suggested when she'd brought it up last time. She knew, with a feeling of trepidation, where the sound was coming from. Although she was afraid, she knew she had to face whatever it was that was troubling her. If it was Richard, she needed to know. She tried to turn on the light but it wasn't working. They were without power again. She felt around for the candle and matches (her eyes were becoming a bit more accustomed to the dark). She lit the candle, but sat up in her bed for a few moments. The sobbing she heard touched her heart. She felt sympathy for whoever it was.

She got out of bed and put on her negligee. She picked up the candle in its holder, and walked to the door. She opened it. The sound was a little louder now, and she turned towards the room at the end of the corridor. That was where it was coming from. She nervously walked towards it. There was a dim light showing underneath the door. When she got there, she inclined her head and listened. Her heart was racing. She straightened up and took hold of the doorknob and opened the door. A dim light came from within. She felt in a daze as she took a step inside. Suddenly her candle flickered violently and blew out. She was not ready for what she saw. The room was completely different. A four-poster bed, not slept in, was against the far wall; all the furnishings from long ago. But what made her blood freeze was the figure at the front window, looking out at the grey dawn, a worn-down candle on the sill. She had half expected it.

Thomas slowly turned a tear-stained face towards her. He stared at her, then said lovingly and hopefully, "Catherine?"

Yvette, in shock, leaned against the door jamb, and put her hand across her mouth, releasing the candle and its holder as she did so. It fell to the floor. She stepped back, breathing heavily, got hold of the doorknob as she moved out of the room, and closed the door. She stood against the wall in disbelief. She thought she was going to faint, but she slid herself along the wall back to her bedroom. She went inside, shut the door and leaned against it. She was trembling as she walked slowly towards her bed and lay down on top of it. Her head was aching. After a while she began to think. Should she wake Richard and tell him what had happened? Would he believe her? Or think she was going mad?

The sobbing had stopped. If she were to go back there now, which she wouldn't, the room would be as it was when Richard showed it to her, and there would be no figure at the window. She was in a turmoil as to what to do. Her head was throbbing now, so she took a couple of aspirin. She went over to the window, drew back the curtains, and opened it slightly. There was a distant rumble of thunder, but dawn had broken. The grey light filled the room, and a slight breeze comforted her and made her feel a little better. After a while she went back to bed, and whether from exhaustion or the aspirin, she fell into a restless sleep. The next thing she knew, someone was knocking on her door, calling her name. It was Richard. She sat up in bed. "Come in," she said.

Richard came into the room, fully dressed and carrying a cup of tea for her. "I was worried about you," he said. "Are you all right?"

Her head still ached and her face was ashen.

"You don't look well," he said. "What's wrong?"

Yvette was going to say, "I'm all right. I'm sorry, I must have overslept." But she didn't. The fact was, she didn't feel well. Her head was still aching despite the aspirin. So she decided to tell Richard just that.

He looked concerned. "I should fetch a doctor."

"No," Yvette replied, "but I think I'll stay in bed a while longer and take another couple of aspirin." Yvette did what she said, and Richard, still concerned, left her to rest. She must have fallen asleep again, because another knock at the door woke her. "Come in," she said, wondering who it might be. It was Richard again.

"I'm sorry to disturb you, my darling, and I hope you don't mind, but I phoned the doctor. He's here now."

Yvette was a little annoyed. She hadn't wanted a doctor, but she could see Richard was worried about her. She sat up and put on her negligee, and ran her hands through her hair. "All right," she said. "If it will make you feel any better, you can ask him to come in."

Richard turned his head and said something to the doctor, who was standing just outside the door. They came in, and Richard introduced them. "Yvette, this is Dr Reed." He turned to the doctor. "Doctor, this is my fiancée, Yvette Moreau."

"Good morning, Miss Moreau."

"Please, call me Yvette," she smiled.

"Very well," he replied kindly. "I believe you've not been feeling very well."

"Oh, it's nothing, really. I'm just a bit tired."

"Shall I go?" asked Richard.

"That's up to Yvette," said the doctor.

"I'd like him to stay," she replied.

"I've been told you've been having quite a few headaches."

"Yes," admitted Yvette. "I've always been prone to them, but just lately they seem to be getting more frequent, and worse."

The doctor pushed up her eyelids and looked at her eyes. "I see." He took out a thermometer and popped it into her mouth. As they waited, the doctor chatted to Yvette. "Richard tells me you lived in France before coming here."

Yvette nodded her head.

"I have a cousin who lives in France – Cannes, as a matter of fact. He loves it, been there 10 years now." A little time later, he took the thermometer out of her mouth and looked at it. "That's normal," he said. Then he checked her heart and pulse. "Everything is as it should be," he said. "Is there anything else bothering you?"

"No, not really," she said, then paused. She may as well mention it, he seemed pleasant enough. "It's just that..." She paused again. "I've been having nightmares."

"Nightmares?" queried the doctor.

"Yes," said Yvette. "And they are so vivid. I don't know if I'm asleep or awake, they are so real."

"Is there something causing these nightmares, d'you think?"

"No," she lied, "not really." How could she tell him? He'd think her mad.

"Have you ever had a head injury of any sort?"

"No," replied Yvette.

"Well, you seem well enough, though a bit pale. What painkillers are you taking?"

"Richard, would you get them please? They're in my dressing table drawer."

Richard walked around the bed to the dressing table, took out the bottle and handed it to the doctor.

He looked at the label. "Yes," he said. "Well, I'll prescribe some different ones, see how you get on with those. What you have to remember is, you've had a lot of changes recently, what with moving to another country, getting used to things here, and of course your wedding is coming up, isn't it?"

"Yes, 28 September," said Yvette.

"29th, darling," corrected Richard, a little surprised she'd got it wrong.

"No, Richard, it's the 28th."

Richard stared at her a moment, and the doctor looked at him. "It's the 29th, Yvette," he repeated. "This coming Friday."

"Oh," said Yvette, looking perplexed.

"I'll tell you what," said the doctor to Yvette. "You see how you get on with the new tablets. I've a feeling this has a lot to do with all the changes you've made recently and, of course, the excitement of the wedding. If, afterwards, you're still having problems, then I'll send you to see a specialist. How's that?" He smiled at her, and squeezed her hand. "I have a feeling though everything will calm down after the wedding."

"All right," smiled Yvette. She gave him her thanks as he left the room with Richard. She was content to leave it at that. After all, the doctor was right, she'd had a number of changes in her life recently. That could account for her headaches and nightmares. They were just vivid dreams. Perhaps she would feel better after the wedding, as the doctor had said. She had a lot to look forward to. She would try to enjoy her life as much as possible. She was lucky, living in a beautiful house, with a man she was very much in love with, and would spend the rest of her life with.

In the hall downstairs, Richard was still worried. He was talking to the doctor. "She will be all right, won't she, doctor?"

"Oh yes," he replied. "Once the wedding is over she'll relax more, and the more she relaxes, the less headaches, and nightmares she'll have. It's just nerves, I'm sure of it."

"I can't believe she got the date of the wedding wrong. I admit 28 September rings a bell with me – I don't know why – but I'd certainly never forget the date of my own wedding."

The doctor put his hand on Richard's shoulder. "Stop worrying. The last thing we want is for you to be ill. As I said, if she doesn't improve after the wedding,

I'll send her to see a specialist, but I'm sure she'll be all right."

Richard took the doctor's hand and shook it. "Thank you, doctor. You've helped put my mind at rest."

"Not at all," smiled the doctor, "not at all."

Richard walked him to the door, and after he'd left he closed the door and stood in the hall, thinking. Why did 28 September seem familiar to him? Then suddenly, it struck him. He walked into his study and got out the paperwork he'd been working on for his book on Thomas and Catherine. He thumbed through the pages, and there it was: Catherine Anne Courtney, born 26 June 1805, died 28 September 1828. The eve of the wedding would be the 100th anniversary of Catherine's death.

Yvette bathed and dressed later that day. She was feeling much better and her headache had gone. She even felt hungry, then remembered she'd not had anything to eat all day, even refusing the lunch Richard had brought her. But now it was as if the rest had done her good. She felt calmer and was ready to accept the explanation the doctor had given her. Even the vision she'd had of Thomas in the bedroom at the end of the corridor was a dream, but it had seemed so real. She walked into the sitting room.

Richard was reading a newspaper. He got up, walked over to her and embraced her. "Darling, it's so good to see you up and about again." Then he looked at her face. "Are you feeling better?"

"Much," smiled Yvette. She sat down on a chair. "I'm glad the doctor came. He was able to put things into perspective. I feel as though a weight has been lifted off me."

"I'm so glad," said Richard, sitting down. "You had me worried."

"Yes, I know. But there's no need to worry about me anymore," she smiled.

Just then, Maurice entered the room and announced dinner was ready to be served.

# Twenty

The following morning, Yvette was up quite early. She had bathed and dressed and was ready to go down to breakfast. She'd had a good night's sleep. The first time, she thought, since she'd arrived at the manor. The talk with the doctor had reassured her. She left her bedroom in high spirits, and went down to the dining room. Richard was already seated, drinking a cup of coffee.

"Good morning" she said as she went to him and kissed his cheek.

He looked up at her and smiled. "You seem a lot better today."

"Yes," answered Yvette, going over to the hot dishes on the sideboard. "I've had a good night's sleep, and feel really well."

"I'm so glad," said Richard. "You had me worried."

"Yes, I know. But there really is no need." She spooned some scrambled egg and tomatoes on to a plate.

Just then, Maurice walked in with more tea and coffee. "Good morning, miss. I trust you are feeling better?"

"Yes, much better, thank you, Maurice," she said as she sat down.

"I'm very pleased to hear it, miss. Would you like tea or coffee this morning?"

"Tea please, but it's all right, I can get it."

"No, not at all, I'll pour it for you," he replied.

"Thank you," she said, buttering a piece of toast.

"Can I refresh your coffee, sir?"

"Yes please," answered Richard.

Maurice poured more coffee into Richard's cup. "Will there be anything else, sir?"

"No, thank you, Maurice."

"Very well, sir," and he left the room.

Richard sipped his coffee then looked at his watch. "Heavens! I shall have to be going, darling." He got up, went over to Yvette and kissed her cheek. "I'm sorry I have to leave you again, but today is the last time I'll be going into the office until after the honeymoon."

"It's all right," said Yvette, "I understand. I'll find something to fill my time."

"I'm glad," he said, stroking her face with the back of his hand. He looked at her and said, "I love you so much." Then he walked over to the door, but before he left the room he turned to her. "'Bye," he said. "See you later"

"'Bye, Richard, and I love you too."

He smiled then closed the door as he left.

Yvette carried on with her breakfast. She heard the car start up and drive away, and had just a moment's feeling of regret that she was alone again. But she finished her breakfast, determined not to lose that initial feeling of happiness she had felt when she got up. She decided to go into the drawing room for a change. It felt quite cool, the fire being laid but not lit. Fresh flowers had been placed on the table. She began to fiddle with them, moving them around slightly where she thought they would look better. She hoped whoever had arranged them initially would not notice, or be hurt.

They hadn't needed rearranging. She realised she was doing it because she was bored already, and Richard had only just left for the office. She looked around the room, then went over to the piano and ran her fingers over the lid. She lifted the piano seat and found various sheets of music, then saw one with which she was familiar: Beethoven's *Für Elise*. She lifted the lid of the piano, sat down and began to play. She was enjoying herself. Her feeling of happiness was coming back to her as she swayed gently to the music. She was nearing the end when there was a knock on the door and Maurice came in carrying envelopes in his hand.

"Excuse me, miss, sorry to disturb you, but I'm just walking down to the post box. Is there anything you would like me to post for you?"

Yvette smiled at his thoughtfulness. "That's very kind of you, Maurice, but there's nothing, thank you."

He smiled, having a little sympathy for her, perhaps sensing her loneliness. "May I say, miss, how well you play the piano?"

Yvette was pleased. "Thank you," she said.

"*Für Elise*, wasn't it?"

"Yes," she smiled. Just then, she winced in pain and held her hand to her head.

Maurice was concerned and walked over to her. "Are you all right, miss?"

She was feeling shaky, but tried to ignore it. "Yes, I'm all right. Just a bit of a headache, that's all."

"Shall I fetch you an aspirin?"

"That's very kind of you, Maurice, but I'm all right, really."

"If you are sure, miss?"

Yvette smiled weakly. "Yes, thank you."

"Very well, miss." He turned to leave the room.

"Oh, Maurice!"

"Yes, miss?"

"Please don't mention this to Richard. He worries. The doctor prescribed me some different tablets, so they should help."

"Very good, miss," and he left the room.

Yvette closed her eyes, then opened them slowly. She looked at the music. It was blurred for a few moments, before she could see it clearly again. After a short while, trying to overcome what had just happened, she began to play again. She imagined how it must have been in past times: a room full of people after dinner, sitting around, listening to Catherine play. She was an accomplished pianist, so Richard had said. Yvette could almost feel the atmosphere in the room, full of guests, enjoying their evening. Yvette stopped playing but she could still hear the music. She listened for a while then her expression turned to anger. She slammed the lid of the piano down. The music stopped. She put her hand to her head, then got up slowly, shakily, and left the room. She walked across the hallway and upstairs. She approached her bedroom, but saw the door was open. Mrs Parker's daughter, Sarah, was making the bed. She stopped as Yvette entered the room.

"I'm sorry, miss, I haven't quite finished. I'm running a little late this morning. Me mum's not feeling too well today, so I'm on my own."

"Oh, I see," said Yvette sympathetically. "I hope it's nothing serious."

"A heavy cold, miss. She'll be right as rain in a day or so."

"I hope so," said Yvette. "Please give her my best wishes."

"That's very kind, miss. I will do." As she smoothed down the quilt she continued. "I'll only be a few minutes – just got to do the dusting – but I can come back later if you prefer?"

"That's all right, Sarah. Don't rush on my account." Yvette turned and left the room. She was feeling a bit better now, and thought she'd go downstairs to the sitting room. The fire would be lit now, and she could rest or read a book. But as she stood in the doorway of her room, she changed her mind. After the nightmare she'd had the night before, she decided she must go into the room at the end of the corridor, the room that would be hers and Richard's after the wedding. She wanted to lay her demons once and for all; prove that it was a normal, but very beautiful, room, and there was nothing to fear. She walked to the door. When she reached it, she hesitated a moment before turning the doorknob. She opened it gradually, her heart racing. She was half expecting the room to be as she'd seen it in her dream, on that cold early morning: the four-poster bed, the candles and Thomas standing by the window. It was still quite vivid in her mind. But, of course, it was the room Richard had shown her, bright and fresh and beautiful. She walked over to the front window and opened it. A slight breeze moved the curtains, and she stood, looking across the lawns and parkland. She smiled at a couple of squirrels scampering over the grass and up a tree. The rooks were cawing overhead. She felt relief. She knew she had been silly. She'd had a bad dream, a very bad dream, but it was over, and what with the new tablets the doctor had prescribed for her, the headaches and nightmares should disappear for good. That is what she hoped for, and felt elated at the thought.

After a few minutes she decided to go downstairs again, and read in the sitting room. She took a step forward towards the door, then stopped. There was something on the floor, by the door. She walked slowly towards it. She stooped and picked it up. It was the candle still in its holder, the one she'd dropped in sheer terror when she had seen Thomas looking out at the grey dawn, weeping.

# Twenty-one

That evening it was clear and warm. A full moon was already up. Outside the front of the manor, there were lights in various windows, and the carriage lamps were on. In the rose garden, at the back of the house, Richard and Yvette were walking, arm in arm, the scent of the roses beautiful in the warmth of the evening.

"I love these warm evenings, don't you?" said Richard.

"Yes," said Yvette.

Richard had noticed she had been subdued during dinner, but had said nothing. "We'll have to make the most of them, though," continued Richard. "The summer's over for this year. We'll not get many evenings like this. We should enjoy them whilst we can."

"Yes," said Yvette. They strolled a little further then suddenly Yvette asked, "Have you asked Benson yet about the summerhouse?"

"Sorry, darling, it completely slipped my mind."

"That's all right, I know you've been busy. But I was thinking, perhaps the land around it could be turned into a rose garden, like this one."

"I don't see why not," said Richard. "But I think Benson will need some help."

"It could be beautiful," continued Yvette, "a summerhouse surrounded by roses. It would be something Thomas and Catherine would have enjoyed – to return it to its former glory."

"I've no idea what it used to look like," said Richard.

"I have an idea," replied Yvette.

"Really?" asked Richard.

"Well," continued Yvette, "I can guess. It would be a lovely place to go to in the warm summer evenings."

"Well, that's true," answered Richard. "But I don't think there's any point starting it now, with winter coming on. Perhaps early next year. I'll ask Benson fairly soon, though. He'll have to arrange for some help besides himself and Joe. Especially restoring the summerhouse. There's not much of it left."

"Yes, of course," smiled Yvette. "Oh, Richard, thank you. You've made me so happy."

"I'm glad," said Richard. They stopped and he looked down at her. "I like to see you happy." They held each other, then kissed.

They continued on their walk, and eventually came to the French windows of the sitting room. The doors were open to the warm summer night, the curtains drawn back, and the light of the room spilling out on to the garden. They went inside and talked to each other for a while. Richard drank a brandy and soda, whilst Yvette had a cup of tea, brought to her by Maurice. The fire was unlit, owing to the warm night. After a while Yvette said she was tired and would go to bed. Richard was surprised – it was still quite early – but they kissed and said goodnight. As she walked to the door Richard said, "D'you know, darling, I've never been as happy as I am tonight."

Yvette smiled at him. "I enjoyed it too." She looked at him, then suddenly, on impulse, ran to him and flung her arms around him.

Richard was taken aback as she hugged him tightly. Then he put his hands on her shoulders, and looked at her. "We'll have many more evenings like this," he said. "We're going to be so happy, you and I. We've got so much to look forward to."

Yvette was trying hard not to break down in tears. She gave him a quick peck on the cheek, then turned so he couldn't see her face as she walked to the door. "Goodnight," she said as she left the room.

"Goodnight," said Richard, looking a little perplexed, as she closed the door behind her.

Yvette walked across the hall and up the stairs. She knew she could hold her tears no longer, and as she entered her bedroom and shut the door, she ran to her bed, sat down on it and began to cry. So intense was her weeping, she worried someone might hear her. After a few minutes, the tears subsided. She dabbed her eyes with a handkerchief, stood up and went to the window, which was open and allowing the beautiful scent of the roses in. She had made her mind up to do something later that night, but she must wait until Richard had gone to bed.

A couple of hours later, she got up, put on her negligee and walked to the door. It was quite dark in the corridor, but she didn't want to put on a light in case Richard noticed it. She hoped he'd be asleep by now. She crept passed his door, and walked silently down the stairs, which were partially lit by the moonlight coming through the window. She was almost down when she slipped and cried out. She stood still for a few moments, hoping no one had heard, then continued on her way

## THE PORTRAIT

across the hall and into the sitting room. Her heart was racing, she was afraid, but if she were to have any peace she must try it. The room was lit quite well by the moonlight, the curtains having been left open, and she walked slowly towards the portrait. She stopped and looked straight into the face of Thomas. She felt she could hardly speak, but she must try.

"Thomas," she said, almost in a whisper, "I hope wherever you are you can hear me. I know you are not at peace, and I understand why. You had a tragic life, and losing your beautiful wife, Catherine, was the end for you. You are still heartbroken and cannot rest. You'd had an argument the very last time you were together. But she loved you as much as you loved her, and still do. It was a dreadful thing to happen, and I don't know how to help you, but I have asked my future husband to have a new summerhouse built, and to have roses, red roses, in the gardens around it. I know how much Catherine loved them. Also I can ask the local vicar to bless it in both your names. I thought by doing this, it would commemorate your love and bring you together again. I hope then you can at last be at rest." She stopped, still looking into the face of Thomas. "I hope it will help you. It breaks my heart to see your torment, but please, Thomas, I beg of you, leave me in peace."

She stood a little while. She felt breathless, her heart still racing. She shivered and clasped her arms about her. Then suddenly the door opened, and the light came on. It was Richard. He looked surprised to see Yvette.

"What are you doing?" he asked.

Yvette searched for an answer. She couldn't tell him she'd been talking to Thomas. What would he think?

Then she moved towards the drinks cabinet. "Oh, I just came down for a drop of brandy. I can't sleep," she lied.

Richard was not convinced. He'd found her looking at the portrait. "I see," he said.

"Yes," said Yvette, smiling. She poured herself a drink. Her hands were shaking slightly, then she walked towards the door where Richard was standing. "I'll take it up to my room and sip it. I've put a drop of soda with it, so I won't fall down drunk," she said, joking, trying to lighten the mood.

"Right," said Richard. "Why didn't you put the light on?"

"The moon was shining in, I didn't need to. I didn't want to disturb anyone."

He stood aside as Yvette walked out of the room. He turned out the light, then, before leaving, he glanced at the portrait, still lit by the moonlight.

As they walked upstairs, Yvette asked, "How did you know I was in the sitting room?"

"I thought I heard something. I got up and when I looked out onto the corridor, I could see your bedroom door was open. You weren't in there, so I just assumed you'd gone into one of the rooms downstairs. The sitting room seemed to be the most likely." Richard stopped at his bedroom.

"Well, goodnight," said Yvette kissing him on the cheek.

"Goodnight," said Richard. "I hope you're able to sleep now."

"So do I," smiled Yvette. "Mrs Gilroy is coming in the morning with my dress."

"I'll see you at breakfast, then," said Richard.

"Yes," she answered, "bright and early."

Richard watched her go into her bedroom and shut the door. Then he went into his own room, shutting the door behind him.

Although Yvette had not wanted the brandy and soda, she drank it. She needed something to calm her nerves. She sat on her bed and began to wonder if Richard had heard her speaking to Thomas. What would he think? She knew he wasn't convinced by what she had told him, and felt sorry having to lie. In some ways she felt foolish, speaking to a ghost. Why had she done it? Would it make any difference? Only time would tell.

The following morning, after breakfast, Richard and Yvette were in the sitting room. Richard was reading a newspaper, Yvette had a book, but she kept glancing at the portrait. Then Maurice came in.

"Excuse me, sir, miss," he said, then to Yvette, "Mrs Gilroy has arrived, miss."

"Oh, good," smiled Yvette, getting up. "Where is she?"

"I asked her to wait in the drawing room, miss."

"Thank you, Maurice," she said, walking to the door.

Richard watched her. He could see she was excited.

She turned to him. "Now don't you come out until I've taken Mrs Gilroy upstairs," she said.

"Righto," smiled Richard.

She went out of the door, closing it behind her. Richard continued to read his paper. Yvette walked into the drawing room. "Mrs Gilroy," she smiled. "How lovely to see you."

"And you, Miss Moreau. I have the dress in the van outside. I'll just fetch it."

"Shall I help you?" asked Yvette.

"That's very kind, but no thank you, I'll be able to manage. I'm used to it."

"Of course," said Yvette. "I'll wait for you here, then we can go up to my room."

Mrs Gilroy went out to her van. Shortly after she came back into the hall carrying, over both arms, the dress and veil, which were protected by a large zipped white bag. Yvette led the way up the stairs and to her room. She closed the door. Her hands were shaking with excitement. She could hardly wait.

Mrs Gilroy hung the dress over the edge of the wardrobe, unzipped the bag and removed it. She laid the veil on the bed. How beautiful the dress looked. It was just what Yvette had wanted. She began to take off her outer garments, whilst Mrs Gilroy unzipped the dress in readiness. After a few moments she helped Yvette put it on. She was almost breathless with excitement. She smoothed her hands over the material. The sleeves were a delicate lace and looked beautiful. She had already bought some shoes and had them ready to put on. Then Mrs Gilroy arranged the veil. When all was complete, Yvette opened the wardrobe door, wherein was a full-length mirror. She turned to face it. A shadow passed momentarily over her face, thinking what had happened the last time she had done this. But the dress remained the same, much to Yvette's relief. She was almost overcome by the beauty of it, turning this way and that. "It's perfect," she said. "Thank you so very much." She gave Mrs Gilroy a kiss on her cheek.

"I'm glad you like it. It's been a pleasure to work on. And what a beautiful bride you will make."

"Thank you," said Yvette. "I feel like a child at Christmas."

"I think, when you're ready, it would be best to bag it up again, and hang it against the wardrobe. That will prevent any creasing and also keep it pristine. It's too long, with the train, to hang inside."

"Yes," agreed Yvette. "Let's do that." She was rather sorry to take it off, but knew she must. Mrs Gilroy helped her, then they both laid it in the bag, along with the veil. Yvette watched as Mrs Gilroy zipped up the bag, and the dress slowly disappeared from view. Then she hooked it over the wardrobe again, whilst Yvette put on her outer clothes.

"Well," smiled Mrs Gilroy, "I'd better be off, I've another fitting later on. But if there is anything else I can help you with, please let me know."

"Don't you want to stay for a cup of tea?" asked Yvette.

"I would love to," replied Mrs Gilroy, "but unfortunately time won't allow it."

"I'll come down with you."

"As you like," smiled Mrs Gilroy, and they both left the room, walking downstairs, and across the hall, chatting all the while. Yvette opened the door. Mrs Gilroy took Yvette's hand and squeezed it. "I hope you both have a wonderful day," she said, kindly.

"Thank you," said Yvette. "Goodbye, and thank you again."

"Goodbye," replied Mrs Gilroy as she walked down the steps, to the van. Yvette watched her as she got in and drove away. Then she went back inside and shut the door. She decided to go into the sitting room, hoping Richard would still be there. He was sitting as before, doing a crossword.

He looked up as Yvette entered the room. He put his paper down and smiled. "Well, how was it?"

"Oh, Richard, it's so beautiful. I can't wait for you to see it."

"Well it won't be long now, darling. I was thinking, after lunch, shall we go for a walk?"

"Yes, I'd like that," said Yvette. She sat on the chair beside the fire, and picked up her book again. Richard carried on with his crossword. She tried not to feel deflated after all the excitement. She was so lucky to have the life she had, and there was so much to look forward to.

In the afternoon, it was sunny but with a threat of rain. Richard and Yvette were walking in the grounds of the manor. There were three horses grazing in a nearby field: Sultan, Bonny and Moonwind. Bonny came up to the fence as they approached; the other two looked up for a moment, then continued grazing. Richard and Yvette walked over to Bonny. They stroked her face and neck, and spoke gently to her. She was enjoying the attention.

"Perhaps," said Yvette, "after the wedding, I could learn to ride. Maybe on Bonny first. She seems so gentle."

"I would like that," said Richard. "I can teach you the rudiments, and I'm sure Barbara would like to be involved. It would give you an interest, and there are some beautiful rides around here."

"I'll look forward to it," smiled Yvette.

A drop of rain fell on Yvette's hand. The sun was still shining but there was a dark cloud overhead, and in a matter of moments the rain began to pour. Richard grabbed Yvette's hand and they ran for cover under a large oak tree. They laughed as they ran. Under the canopy of the tree, it was dry.

"I didn't expect that," said Richard.

"No," replied Yvette. "The horses aren't bothered, are they?" She looked across at the field. Bonny had joined the others and was grazing again. Richard looked at her smiling face, and with his hand under her chin, gently lifted her face towards his. They looked at one another before kissing passionately. Some distance off, Thomas, in the pouring rain, was watching, saddened by what he saw.

# Twenty-two

Late that night, Yvette was asleep in bed. The fire in her room had been lit that evening, but was now only embers. The curtains and window were partly open. She turned restlessly as she began to dream. *Someone (Yvette imagined in her dream to be Catherine) was on horseback, cantering along a track in a wood. Suddenly she noticed something moving in the trees. She reined in her horse and came to a standstill. She smiled as she saw a small deer in the trees. Then she saw something else. There were two men with guns, hiding in the bushes. She saw one of them take aim on the deer. She shouted out a warning. The deer instantly ran away. Then the two men looked across at her, and the one who had taken aim on the deer now focused on Catherine. Angry, he fired a shot just over her head. Instantly her horse whinnied and reared up, throwing her to the ground. The two men ran over to her. They looked down anxiously, thinking what the consequences would be if they were caught. The man who had fired the gun looked around to see if anyone had witnessed what had happened, but no one was there. He pulled his friend away. She heard them arguing about what they should do. It seemed the other man wanted to stay and help her, but after a few moments, he was pulled into the wood by the other, and they ran away.*

## THE PORTRAIT

*She looked up into the branches above her, the sun glinting through. Her horse was standing nearby, grazing. Then things blurred, and she passed out. She lay there a long time, in and out of consciousness. Then it was dark. It was the moon that now shone through the trees. Suddenly she heard voices. It was a search party. Blurred lights were coming towards her. As they got nearer, they became clearer, and she saw faces looking down at her. They were troubled by what they saw. The last thing she remembered was a bright light from one of the lanterns, as they bent down to help her. Then everything went black, as she fell again into unconsciousness.*

*Back at the chateau she was in bed. She had a bandage around her head and was lying quite still. She opened her eyes and could see Thomas kneeling beside the bed, looking anxiously at her. There was a doctor also by her bedside, and her parents were at the end of the bed, her mother weeping. Catherine was in a lot of pain. She tried to turn her head, but couldn't. She could see the window, looking out on the moonlit night, and a candle on the sill. The fire was lit and flickered on the walls and ceiling. A couple of lanterns were lit on the tables nearby. She glanced from Thomas to her mother and father. Tears welled in her eyes as she saw her mother weeping. Then she looked at Thomas again. Tears trickled down his face, and she weakly lifted her hand to his cheek, and wiped them away. He clasped her hand and kissed it.*

*The doctor and her mother and father moved away from the bed so Thomas could be alone with his wife. Catherine looked at his face and tried to smile. He held her hand with both of his, hoping to give her comfort.*

*She glanced to the window again and saw the moon in the dark sky, so beautiful. Then she winced with pain. Thomas clenched her hand tighter, as if it could help her. Then he said quietly:*

*"My dearest love, please forgive me. We should never have argued. I am so very sorry. I do love you so much."*

*She seemed to settle for a few moments, then she cried out in pain. The doctor and her parents returned to the bedside. As Catherine looked at Thomas, his face began to blur. She no longer recognised him, and she became anxious, pulling her hand away from his. He was distraught.*

*"Catherine, Catherine," he said over and over.*

*She glanced once more through the window, then took her final breath, and could see no more. Thomas was heartbroken.*

*"I love you, Catherine, I love you," he called out, tears running down his face.*

*Her spirit looked down at the scene. Thomas held his dear wife's hand, and wept. Her mother and father were sobbing, and the doctor stood beside the bed looking down at her. On the windowsill, the candle flickered violently, then went out.*

Yvette turned restlessly in her sleep, and continued to dream. *Now she was in a churchyard. It was a little misty and damp. Thomas, and Catherine's mother and father, were standing beside her grave, whilst the rest of the mourners stood nearby. The priest was speaking and they all had their heads bowed. Suddenly, a breeze came from nowhere and blew in Thomas's face. He stepped nearer the grave and dropped a single red rose onto her coffin.*

*"My dearest love, how will I live without you?"*

Suddenly Yvette woke up, deeply troubled by her dream. Then her eyes grew wide as she saw a figure standing at the foot of the bed. She sat up, afraid. After a moment she reached out and turned on the bedside lamp. There was no one there. She lay back on her pillows, leaving the light on. Her head was aching again. She got up and went over to the dressing table, and sat down. Out of the drawer, she took a couple of the tablets the doctor had prescribed her. She swallowed them with a glass of water, then looked at herself in the mirror. Was the face in her dream her own? She put her head in her hands. She was disappointed she was still having bad dreams. Maybe it would take a while for the tablets to work? She'd only been using them a couple of days. She turned and looked at her dress hanging from the wardrobe. Maybe that is what she had seen when she woke up. She preferred to think so.

She looked at her reflection again. She was pale and had started to get shadows under her eyes. *A fine bride I'm going to make*, she thought. After the wedding, if things didn't improve, she would ask the doctor if she could see a specialist; someone who would understand and help to put an end to her vivid and frightening dreams.

# Twenty-three

The next morning in the sitting room, Richard was sitting by a roaring fire, reading his newspaper. Yvette walked in.

*This must be his routine when he's not going to the office*, she thought.

He looked up when she walked in. "Hello, darling," he said cheerfully. "What have you been doing with yourself? You've been gone ages."

Yvette wandered over to the window and stared out. "I hope you won't be cross, Richard."

"Cross?" he asked. "I could never be cross with you. What is it?"

"I've just been on the phone to Barbara," she said.

"Oh?" he asked.

"Yes. I've told her I won't be staying with them on the eve of the wedding."

Richard put down his newspaper. "You won't? Why on earth not?"

"Because I'd rather stay here. If you don't mind, that is?"

"Of course I don't mind, this is your home. I just don't see why. I thought it was all settled."

"I know," said Yvette.

"So you'll be leaving for the church from here, after all?"

"No. Barbara said she'd pick me up early on the morning and take me to Flaxted Hall. I can get ready and leave for the church from there."

"I see," said Richard, wondering why she'd changed her mind. "I hope Barbara wasn't too disappointed. I know how much she was looking forward to you staying."

"I'd rather be here, where you are. I think I'd feel easier in my mind. She was very nice about it." Yvette turned from the window and walked over to the other armchair, and sat down. "She said she understood. We'll still be having dinner there that night."

"Well of course, darling. If you're sure that's what you want."

"Yes, I am," she smiled. "Quite sure."

Two nights later, on the eve of the wedding, Richard and Yvette were travelling up the driveway of Flaxted Hall. The wind was blowing quite hard, and there was a distant rumble of thunder. As they neared the house, lights in many windows could be seen, and the carriage lamps were lit either side of the huge wooden door. As they got out of the car, the door opened and Reginald came out to greet them.

"Hello, you two," he said jovially. "Come inside, out of this weather." They walked through the door into the hall, a big room with paintings on the walls and a large mirror in a golden frame. There was a table by the stairs, with a beautiful flower display upon it. Barbara was standing just inside. She put her arms around Yvette and gave her a kiss on the cheek.

"Hello, my dear, how lovely to see you. And Richard, of course," she said, as she kissed him also.

Their butler, Matthew, came to take their coats.

"It's blustery out there," said Richard.

"Yes, we'll have a storm tonight, no doubt," commented Reginald.

"As long as it's all right for tomorrow," added Barbara.

Yvette smiled as they walked into the sitting room. This too was a large room, but felt cosy with a roaring fire, set around which were chairs and a settee, and antique furniture was placed tastefully here and there. On the rug in front of the fire sat a dog, a black and white springer spaniel. He was quite old, and got up, wagging his tail slowly as he ambled towards them.

"Oh," said Reginald, "how remiss of me. This is Rufus, head of the household," he joked.

Both Richard and Yvette bent down and stroked the top of his head and long ears.

"Fifteen this year," said Barbara. "He's done very well."

"He's had a good life," said Richard.

"He certainly has," said Reginald. Then he turned to Richard and Yvette. "You'll have a drink?" he asked. "Yvette, what would you like?"

"Just a small brandy and soda, thank you," she replied, sitting down on the settee. Richard sat beside her.

"And for you, Richard?" continued Reginald.

"The same, please," he answered.

Reginald went to the drinks cabinet and Barbara sat down in an armchair. Rufus curled up again on the rug, and in no time at all he was snoring and twitching in his sleep.

"So," said Barbara, smiling, "everything set for tomorrow?"

"Yes," smiled Richard. "I hope so, anyway."

"Here we are," said Reginald, handing a drink first to Yvette and then to Richard. He went back to fetch his and Barbara's drinks. "'Here we are, old girl," he said, handing it to her. He held his glass in a toast. "To Yvette and Richard. I hope you will be as happy as we have been."

"Hear hear!" agreed Barbara.

They held their glasses up and then took a drink.

"Isn't this nice?" said Barbara. "All together again."

They chatted for a while, then Matthew entered, and announced dinner was served. They all stood up and walked through to the dining room. Another beautiful room, with a fire blazing, and a table set with a white cloth, shining silver cutlery and crystal glasses. There was a floral decoration of white and red roses in the centre. They all sat in their places, Reginald and Barbara at each end, with Richard and Yvette across from each other. They chatted comfortably during the meal, and the wine complimented the food beautifully. A little later, Matthew entered the room and went over to the sideboard, on which stood an ice bucket containing a champagne bottle. Matthew removed the cork with a slight *pop*.

"Champagne," smiled Richard. "You're spoiling us."

Matthew moved to each person in turn and poured. He put the bottle back in the ice bucket and left the room.

Barbara stood up, glass in hand, and the others followed her lead. "To Richard and Yvette," she said. "May they have many years of happiness."

"To Richard and Yvette," smiled Reginald.

They all raised their glasses and then drank. After a few moments they sat down and continued their conversation. It was during the sweet course that the conversation took a turn for the worst. It was started with a question from Richard:

"Did you buy Lord Maybury's mare?" he asked.

"Of course he did," said Barbara, looking across at Reginald. "He'd decided to buy her before he'd even tried her."

"And is she as good as you thought?" asked Richard.

Reginald had finished his sweet, and patted his mouth with his napkin. "Even better," he said. "And she's fast too."

Barbara looked across at Reginald. "Yes. Had a bit of trouble pulling her up yesterday, didn't you?" she said.

"She's just a bit headstrong, that's all," he replied, trying to play it down.

"Headstrong?" said Barbara. She looked at Richard and Yvette. "She had me worried, I can tell you."

Reginald took another sip of his champagne. "Oh, I managed all right."

"She's too much for you, Regi," said Barbara, seriously concerned. "That's probably why he was selling her. You're all I've got. I don't want you having an accident and hurting yourself or, even worse, getting killed."

Yvette had been listening to all this whilst sipping her champagne. Then suddenly she said, "Catherine was killed in a riding accident." Everyone turned to look at her. Then Yvette continued as if in a daze. "She didn't die straight away, but later that night." Then she looked directly at them all. "Tonight is the 100th anniversary of her death."

Richard stared at her.

"Is it really, my dear?" said Barbara, feeling a little uncomfortable, wondering why Yvette should mention such a thing. Then Barbara turned to Reginald. "Well, there you are, riding isn't the safest of sports. You should be looking for something a little quieter, Regi, at your age." She turned to Richard. "I was only saying to Yvette the other day, he refuses to mellow. By the way," said Barbara turning to Yvette, "I meant to tell you. After I dropped you off the other day, the strangest thing happened. I was going back along the drive, not travelling very fast, as luck would have it. I must have been about halfway down, when a man stepped out in front of me. He seemed to appear from nowhere. Of course I slammed on the brakes, but he just stared at me blankly. He didn't seem bothered that I'd almost knocked him down. Anyway, I drove on a few yards, then stopped. I got out of the car and looked around, and d'you know, he'd disappeared. Not a sign of him. It was most odd. If I didn't know any better, I'd swear I'd seen a ghost," she laughed.

Just then there was a clatter as Yvette dropped her glass, which still had a small amount of champagne in it. She was embarrassed and flustered. Barbara got up to help her. Richard looked concerned, knowing what had upset her. Reginald sensed something was wrong, by the concern in Richard's face.

"Shall I ring for Matthew?" asked Reginald.

"There's no need," said Barbara, dabbing at Yvette's dress and the tablecloth. "Are you all right, my dear?"

"Yes," said Yvette. "I'm so sorry."

"No need to apologise. Let me get you some more champagne," said Barbara, walking over to the ice bucket.

"Oh, no thank you," said Yvette. "I had drunk most of it. I better not have any more, what with the wine as well."

"Are you sure?" asked Barbara.

"Yes, I'm sure."

"Would anyone else like a top up?" asked Barbara.

"I wouldn't mind," said Richard.

"And me." Reginald held up his glass.

Moments later Barbara sat down, and the matter of the little incident was forgotten. As they began to chatter again, there was a flash of lightning which made the lights flicker, then a rumble of thunder, quite close by.

"Here it comes," said Reginald.

Barbara looked at Yvette. "These two will be starting on the cigars and port in a minute. What say we go through to the drawing room? We'll be more comfortable in there. I'll have Matthew bring us some coffee."

"Yes, all right," smiled Yvette.

They stood up to leave the room. The men got up as well, as a matter of courtesy. Richard noticed Yvette was looking ill at ease. He walked over to her, took her hand, and kissed it. "See you in a little while, darling."

She smiled at him, then left the room with Barbara.

The two men sat down again, and Reginald took up a decanter of port and poured for Richard. "Not too much for me," said Richard. "I've got to keep a clear head for tomorrow."

## THE PORTRAIT

After filling his own glass, Reginald offered Richard a cigar. He took one, and Reginald gave him a light. They both sat there smoking, then Reginald said, "Barbara is very taken with your young lady."

"Yes, I know," smiled Richard. "It's good to see them getting on so well."

"She's thrilled to be involved with the wedding," said Reginald, "especially as she has no children of her own upon whom to lavish her attention."

They were silent for a while, enjoying their cigars, then Reginald said, "A bit like old times, this."

Richard smiled, but was thinking back to the earlier conversation about Catherine's riding accident. Reginald noticed his pensive manner, and said:

"Don't think I'm prying, but there's nothing wrong, is there?"

"Wrong?" queried Richard.

"You're looking a little thoughtful, old boy, that's all."

Richard looked at his cigar, abstractedly turning it with his fingers. He was wondering whether to confide in Reginald, and decided he must confide in someone. "It's Yvette," he said.

"Yvette?" asked Reginald, surprised.

"I don't know what it is, but there's something troubling her. I've asked her about it, but she says there's nothing wrong."

"Well, maybe there isn't," said Reginald, taking a sip of port.

"Oh, there is, I can tell. She's been acting so strangely, and she seems to have become obsessed with the story of Thomas and Catherine. Well, you heard her tonight.

What a thing to say. It was morbid." He took a drink. He suddenly felt a little guilty. "Perhaps I shouldn't be telling you this. It seems disloyal."

"No," said Reginald. "You're right to tell me, if it helps. It won't go any further, I promise you."

Richard abstractedly brushed ash from his cigar onto an ashtray, then continued. "Some strange things have happened since we came home – things I can't explain – and there's been some upset. Now she seems to be on edge all the time."

"Yes," said Reginald, "I had noticed. And I could tell something was troubling you."

"Do you know what she wants to do now?" He paused, then looked at Reginald. "To rebuild an old summerhouse in an overgrown area of the garden, and surround it with rose bushes."

"But that sounds a nice idea," said Reginald.

"Well, maybe it is, but I feel there is more to it than that."

"Like what?" asked Reginald.

"It's the kind of thing Thomas would have done for Catherine. It would have been him who had it built in the first place, I wouldn't doubt. I feel she wants it to be some sort of shrine. Then she says she's seen a man hanging around. You saw her reaction tonight when Barbara said she'd seen someone. Sometimes she'll focus her attention on something or somebody in the distance, but when I turn around, there's no one there. She seems in a dreamlike state when she does it."

"Did you tell the doctor when he called?" asked Reginald.

"No, I didn't. Perhaps I should have done. I didn't want him to think there was something mentally wrong with her, because I'm sure there isn't. It's just that, in the short time she's been at Shearwater, she's become like a flower that's lost its bloom." Just then, the lights flickered again as the storm got nearer. Rain started lightly at first, but then lashed at the windows.

"Has the doctor given her anything to take that might help?"

"Just some different painkillers, stronger than the ones she'd been taking. She's been getting a lot of headaches recently. She had one this afternoon, as a matter of fact. I was almost going to cancel tonight, but she insisted on coming."

"It's probably just wedding nerves."

"That's what the doctor said. But it's more than that. The other night I thought I'd heard something. I got up and went to investigate. Her bedroom door was open, but she was not there. I went downstairs to find her in the living room, in the dark, looking at the portrait. I think I took her by surprise, and she told me she hadn't been able to sleep, and had come down for a nightcap. I know it seems awful to say, but I didn't believe her. I just wish she'd confide in me. I am to be her husband, after all."

Reginald topped up Richard's glass, then his own. "You know, Richard, it must have been very hard for her leaving everything behind, and coming to live in a strange country. It takes some nerve, and perhaps she's lonely, too."

"Yes, I know," agreed Richard.

"Obviously," continued Reginald, "you can't be there all the time, you've your business to run. But she was saying to Barbara, only the other day, she hopes you'll be entertaining more, after the wedding."

"She said that?" asked Richard. He thought about it a moment then said, "She's never given me the impression she was that keen on entertaining. She seemed to have very few friends in France."

"And she has no family?" queried Reginald.

"Her parents were killed when she was quite young, and her aunt looked after her. When she died some years later, Yvette moved to the town where I met her, and had a job in a dress shop there. She's had to make her own way in life."

"Poor girl," said Reginald. "So she had no one?"

"No one close," said Richard. "That's why I thought it would be quite easy for her to make a new life over here. She was a little subdued and thoughtful sometimes, even in France. I flattered myself I could make her happy. How wrong I was. She's worse now than she was then."

"Try to be patient, Richard. Give her time. She's a lovely young woman, and you're a very lucky man."

"Yes, I know."

"I'm sure when the wedding's over, she'll settle down into married life."

Richard looked a little unsure.

"You know," said Reginald, trying to lighten the mood, "you've started tongues wagging."

"Oh?" said Richard, perplexed. "Why?"

"Returning home and living in the same house with a young French woman."

Richard smiled. "We are engaged."

"You know what they're like around here," said Reginald. "Any little piece of gossip."

"Who cares?" said Richard. "After tomorrow they won't have anything to gossip about, will they?"

"That's the ticket," smiled Reginald. He held up his glass of port. "All the very best to you, my dear fellow. I'm sure you'll both be very happy."

Richard picked up his glass. "Thanks, Regi. I hope so." He finished his port.

Just then they heard piano music coming from the drawing room. "Ah, just listen to that," smiled Reginald.

"Barbara plays beautifully," said Richard.

"She certainly does. Shall we go through?"

"Yes, why not," said Richard stubbing out the remainder of his cigar.

They both got up and walked towards the door. Then Richard stopped. "Oh, by the way, before I forget, I'd better give you this." Richard took something from his pocket. "The wedding ring," he smiled, and opened the box.

Reginald whistled softly. "Beautiful," he said.

"Take care of it, or there won't be a wedding tomorrow," joked Richard.

Reginald took the box. "Don't worry, old boy," he said, putting the ring in his pocket, "it'll be perfectly safe with me."

They both left the room, and walked across the hall to the drawing room, the music becoming louder. Inside the room, the fire was burning brightly, the curtains closed against the storm. Both men stopped and stared, for it was Barbara sitting in the armchair, near the fire, and Yvette who was playing. She hadn't noticed the door opening and the two men coming in, and she continued to play, Beethoven's *Moonlight Sonata*. Her body swayed as she played, and Richard stood, pleasantly surprised by what he saw. Barbara smiled at them, but put a finger to her lips, wishing them to remain silent.

They both sat down until the last note was played. Then they clapped. Yvette turned around, surprised they were there. She smiled. Richard was almost overcome with pride. He felt a lump in his throat. Then he said quietly, "I didn't know you could play the piano, and so well."

"I learnt when I was a little girl, my aunt helped me. And I also had lessons."

"Well," said Barbara, "you play beautifully, my dear."

"Hear, hear," agreed Reginald.

Yvette walked over to the settee and sat down next to Richard, a happy smile on her face.

Richard gave her a kiss on the cheek. "Well done, darling."

The storm was now raging outside. Rain battered against the windows and there was thunder and lightning simultaneously. The storm was right overhead. Suddenly the lights went out. "Oh blast," said Reginald.

"Regi!" scolded Barbara. "We have company."

"Oh yes, sorry."

Some moments later the lights came back on again. "Ah, there we are," smiled Barbara.

But the lights continued to flicker every time there was a flash of lightning. Yvette looked nervous; she was clasping her hands around her arms.

"Are you all right, Yvette?" asked Barbara.

She didn't answer.

"Are you cold?" she asked. "Come and sit nearer the fire."

Still no answer.

Richard looked at her. "Darling, Barbara's talking to you."

After a moment, she came to herself again. "Oh, I'm so sorry," she said.

"Would you like to come nearer the fire?" asked Barbara.

"No," she smiled. "I'm all right, thank you."

Richard and Reginald looked knowingly at each other.

"Would you like another cup of coffee?" asked Barbara.

"No, thank you," replied Yvette.

"A brandy?" asked Reginald. "That'll warm you up."

"No, I'm fine, really."

"What about you, Richard? Would you like a brandy?"

"No thanks, but I'll have a cup of coffee, if I may?"

Barbara got up and poured the coffee, and handed it to him.

"Thanks," said Richard.

There was now tension in the room. Even Barbara had noticed it because she looked at Reginald, perplexed.

Richard drank his coffee, then said, "Perhaps we should be going soon."

"But it's still quite early," said Barbara, disappointed.

"It's been a great evening," lied Richard, for it had, indeed, been spoilt. "We've got a big day tomorrow," he smiled. "It might be best to go, in case the storm gets worse. There may be flooding on the roads."

"You could stay the night, both of you," said Barbara.

"That's very kind," said Richard, "but I think it's best if we go home. All our things for tomorrow are at the manor." They both got up from the settee.

Barbara pulled the cord to fetch Matthew. "Would you get their coats please, Matthew?" said Barbara when he entered the room.

"Of course, madam," he replied, and went to fetch them.

They all walked out into the hall, and stood chatting whilst Matthew brought the coats, and helped to put them on.

Barbara took Yvette's hand and looked at her with concern. "Are you sure you're all right?"

"Yes," said Yvette. "Please don't worry about me, there really is no need. But I do want to thank you both for a lovely evening."

"It's been a pleasure," smiled Barbara.

"Yes, indeed," agreed Reginald.

Barbara still felt there was something wrong, but put it out of her mind. She gave Yvette a kiss on the cheek. "Goodnight, my dear. Sleep well. I'll pick you up about 7.30am."

"Goodbye, Barbara," said Yvette, then she went to Reginald and gave him a kiss on the cheek. "Goodbye," she said. "And thank you both for all your kindness."

Richard said his goodbyes. Then Matthew appeared with an umbrella.

"I'll see you both to the car, sir, or you'll be soaked."

They thanked him, and he opened the door. The rain was still pouring, and there were flashes of lightning. He put up the umbrella, and escorted them to the car. He opened the doors for them both. Richard gave a quick wave to Reginald and Barbara, before he got in.

"Thank you, Matthew," he said.

"Not at all, sir."

Matthew went back inside, leaving Barbara and Reginald standing in the doorway. Yvette looked at them through the car window, and smiled. Suddenly she felt emotional, and turned away.

They both waited in the doorway until the car moved down the drive, then looked at each other as they walked back inside, and shut the door. Inside, Barbara said, "There's something wrong, isn't there? Did Richard mention anything?"

Reginald remembered his promise to Richard, that he'd keep their conversation to himself. "It's just wedding nerves, I expect," he smiled. "There's nothing to worry about." Barbara was not convinced, so Reginald put his arm around her. "Come on, old girl, I could do with a nightcap."

In the car Richard and Yvette were travelling along in silence. Richard was still concerned, wondering what was wrong, but trying not to let it show. "It was a lovely meal, wasn't it?" he said.

"Yes, it was," answered Yvette. "I'm so glad you have the Applebys as friends."

"They're your friends now, as well, darling. They think a lot of you, and we'll have some good times together, you'll see."

The storm was moving away and clouds scurried across the sky. By the time they reached the manor, a full moon was shining, lighting up the house and the grounds. It had gone quite still after the fury of the storm. There were no lights on in the house. Not even the carriage lamps were lit.

"Oh no!" said Richard.

"What's wrong?" asked Yvette.

"I think the power's out again."

"Oh," she said.

Richard stopped the car outside the manor. He helped Yvette out, and they walked up the steps to the door. The moon was bright, and shone down, illuminating the scene. Maurice was in his quarters, as he wasn't expecting them back so early. Richard opened the door, but Yvette turned around and looked across the lawns and parkland. A low mist was starting to form. Nearby an owl hooted. It looked like an enchanted place. She breathed in the air. "What a beautiful night," she said, and walked inside. Richard closed the door.

There were several candles dotted about the hall, flickering on the walls and paintings, giving it an almost medieval effect. Just then Maurice appeared, candle in hand.

"Oh, good evening, sir, miss. I didn't think you'd be back just yet. I trust you had a pleasant evening." He placed his candle on a nearby table.

"Yes, thank you, Maurice," said Richard, as he and Yvette took off their coats.

"That was some storm, wasn't it?" said Maurice, taking the coats from them.

"That's why we thought it may be best to leave early. In case of flooding."

"Indeed, sir," said Maurice. "I'll light the candles in the sitting room for you."

"It's all right, Maurice," said Richard, "I'll do it."

"As you wish, sir. Will there be anything else?"

Richard looked at Yvette. "Would you like some tea, darling?"

"No, thank you," she smiled.

"Then that's all, thank you, Maurice. We won't be needing anything else tonight. You may as well have an early night. It's going to be a big day for us all tomorrow."

"Yes indeed, sir. All the staff will be here to help. They're all very excited, and they've asked me to pass on their very best wishes to you both, to which, of course, you can add my own."

"That's very kind," said Richard. "Isn't it, darling?"

"Yes," agreed Yvette, smiling. "Very kind."

"Well then, I'll say goodnight, sir, miss."

"Goodnight," they both answered.

Richard made for the sitting room. "Come on, darling, let's have a nightcap."

"Yes, all right," she answered. "But I just need to go to my room first."

"I'll pour you a drink," said Richard. "What would you like?"

"Just a small brandy, thank you." She picked up a candle from one of the tables in the hall, and walked upstairs, casting a shadow on the walls as she went. She walked towards her bedroom, just glancing at the door at the end of the corridor. Then she walked into her room, put the candle down and sat on the bed. There was a small fire burning in the grate. After a moment she went over to the dressing table, sat on the stool, and looked at herself in the mirror. She looked down and rested her head in her hands. After a few moments she took out her painkillers, and took a couple. She brushed her hair, feigned a smile on her lips, and then went down to the sitting room.

As she walked in, Richard was sitting on the settee with his brandy. He'd lit several candles around the room, and there was a good fire burning in the grate. He had poured Yvette's drink, and had put it on a small table next to the settee. She walked over and sat down beside him.

"You all right?" asked Richard.

"Yes," smiled Yvette. She sipped her brandy but Richard could see, as fine as gossamer, anxiety on her face. She glanced at the portrait. Richard saw her.

"You're much taken with that portrait, aren't you?" he smiled, trying not to cause upset, but wanting desperately to know what was causing her concern.

After a moment she said, "Do you believe a person can have lived before, in another time?" She looked at Richard.

His smile faded, and he said solemnly, "No, I don't."

Yvette turned to look at the portrait again.

"You know," continued Richard, "when I told you the story of Thomas and Catherine, I didn't think you'd take it so much to heart, or I'd never have said anything."

"Why?" asked Yvette.

"It's just that you seem to have become a little obsessed with it. Certainly since you've come here, there's been something troubling you. I just wish you would tell me what it is."

Yvette felt uneasy. She looked down at her drink.

"Please," implored Richard. "Nothing you could tell me would make a difference to the way I feel about you. I just want you to be happy, that's all. I hate to see you troubled like this. It's the eve of our wedding, we should be celebrating."

"You'll mock me when I tell you," said Yvette.

"I wouldn't do that," he said indignantly. "What do you take me for?"

"Then I'll tell you," she said. She put her glass down on the table. "It is said Thomas blamed himself for Catherine's death, but he should not have done." Yvette was remembering her dream. "On the last day of her life, the argument between herself and Thomas was not over some trivial matter, as some believed, but over something very dear to them both." She turned her gaze to the portrait again. "It is said Catherine lost her first child during pregnancy. That is true, but she desperately wanted another. Thomas feared for her health, and thought it best to wait a while, he loved her so much. But she was angry. She rushed from the room and decided to go for that fateful ride. She was not riding recklessly, as some thought. She had spotted two men in the wood, about to shoot a small deer. She frightened the deer away, and was happy because she had saved its life. But the men were angry. One of them raised his gun towards her, and fired over her head, but her horse reared in fright, and she was thrown."

Richard was looking at Yvette in astonishment at what he was hearing.

Yvette continued: "There was a sickening thud, sharp pain, then, moments later, the shadow of the two men standing over her. She thought they'd come to help, but they turned and left her lying there." Yvette paused then looked into Richard's eyes. "All these things I remember," she paused again, then came the biggest shock to Richard, "because *I* was Catherine. How else could I know?"

Richard looked at her incredulously, and took her hand, anxious for her. "Listen, darling," he said. "I know you've been troubled by the story of Thomas and Catherine, but I never realised just how much.

I've heard people who claim they've lived before, in some other life, but I don't believe it. It just isn't possible."

Yvette was disappointed and saddened by Richard's reaction. She had wanted to confide in him, but it was a mistake.

"You've a very vivid imagination, that's all. It accounts for all your bad dreams – it's been playing on your mind. But you must stop dwelling on it." Then, trying to lighten the mood, he said, "You should try writing. I'd publish you any time."

It was the wrong thing to say. Yvette pulled her hand away from him, stood up and went over to the fireplace. "You said you wouldn't mock me," she said.

"I'm not mocking you, darling. We all have strange dreams at times, and because you're thinking about the story, you're having very vivid ones. Come and sit down."

Yvette went back to him and sat down. He took her hand and kissed it. "You've been very lonely since you got here, haven't you?"

Yvette knew it was true, but it wasn't the issue here.

"The trouble is," he continued, "you've had too much time on your hands. But things will change, I promise. You'll make new friends. We'll have people round, there'll be parties, and I'll be able to see more of you when I make Fotheringay a partner. There'll be children too, in time."

Yvette was close to tears, and went to the window. She drew back the curtains, and the moonlight shone through.

Richard turned to her. "You'll see, darling, we'll be so very happy."

Yvette tried to fight back her tears. "You've made everything possible for me, Richard, and I'm so grateful. But I've given you nothing in return."

"Except yourself," smiled Richard. "And that means everything to me." He walked over to her, and turned her towards him. He saw she had tears in her eyes and felt sympathy for her. "Everything will be all right, darling, you'll see." A tear rolled down her cheek and Richard brushed it away. He kissed her.

"I want you to finish your book on Thomas and Catherine. I believe you'll be able to now," she said.

Richard was a little annoyed that she still believed what she had told him. He went to speak, but she put her finger on his lips to stop him. "Maybe I've given you something after all," she smiled. She looked at his face, then hugged him tightly. She looked at Thomas's portrait, lit by the fire beneath it. "I am going to be so very happy, believe me," she said.

Richard looked at her. He was perplexed by her manner. She smiled at him. Then he said slowly, "I won't be seeing you again, will I?"

Her smile faded. "No," she said.

"Until we meet in church tomorrow, I mean," said Richard.

She kissed him lightly on the cheek, and walked towards the door.

Richard was troubled. "Goodnight, darling," he said. "I'll see you in the morning, at the church."

She looked at him, then walked from the room. As she closed the door behind her, she said softly, "Goodbye."

# Twenty-four

Yvette walked with a candle up to her bedroom. She closed the door and put the candle down. She walked over to the window, drew back the curtains and opened the window slightly. She was overwhelmed by the beauty of the scene below. The moon overhead cast its light over the garden; the scent of the roses, after the rain, was heady. She gazed around, as if seeking someone, but there was no one there. After a while, she changed into her nightdress, and lay on top of the bed, her arm across her eyes. She could hear the fox barking, somewhere in the parkland, and an owl screeched nearby, as if in reply. It was only 10.15, but she knew something was going to happen, before the night was over. She felt different – she didn't feel afraid. Her head was still aching, but she didn't want to take any more tablets. She turned on her side, and eventually fell asleep.

She didn't know what made her wake up, but she'd only been asleep for half an hour. She knew she needed to get up. She tried the bedside lamp, but the electricity was still out. She got up from her bed and put on her negligee. She lit another candle, and left the room. As she walked along the corridor, she could just make out a flickering light beneath Richard's bedroom door. He had decided on an early night. In fact, he was in bed, lying on his back, his eyes open, deep in thought. Then

## THE PORTRAIT

he blew out the candle, turned on his side, and tried to sleep. Yvette saw the light go out and walked slowly past his door, and down the stairs, the candle lighting her way.

She went into the sitting room. The fire was still lit, and Yvette walked over to it, and looked up at the portrait. Thomas's figure flickered in the candlelight. She gazed into his eyes a moment, then put the candle down on the table by the settee, and sat down. She was feeling very tired; her head pounded with pain. She put her legs up onto the settee and rested her head against the arm rest. After a while, she fell asleep. Not long after, she woke, and felt strangely at ease. She had a sudden feeling of overwhelming happiness. Her head was not aching anymore. In fact, she felt better than she had ever felt.

She got up and walked over to the French windows. The curtains were still open. She opened the doors on to the garden. The moon shone down, lighting the scene with its beauty. She looked at the cherub at the end of the garden, and the shrubs and roses in the borders. Suddenly she saw something, just a movement across the lawn. Someone was standing there. She stepped forward, then stopped. She was not frightened, she knew who the figure was, and she held out her arms as he moved towards her. As he got closer, she could see his handsome face – not as it had been on the other occasions. He was not rough or unkempt, but dressed in his finery, just as he was in the portrait. He had a red rose in his hand, and as he reached her, he offered it to her, and she took it. They embraced as though they would never let go of each other. Then after a few moments, they kissed.

In his bedroom, Richard woke suddenly. He felt ill at ease, and sat up in bed. He was worrying about Yvette, and what she had said to him earlier. He lit his candle, put on his dressing gown, and opened the door of his bedroom. He glanced towards Yvette's room and could see the door was open. Curious, he walked towards it, and looked through the door. He could see the bed was empty and, after scanning the room, saw she wasn't there.

He went to the room at the end of the corridor, thinking she may have gone in there, but as he opened the door, he saw, in the moonlight spilling out over the room, she was not there either. He closed the door, then thought for a moment. He decided to go downstairs. Maybe she had gone for a drink to help her sleep, what with the excitement of the wedding.

He entered the sitting room. The French windows were closed, but the curtains were still open. He glanced around the room, then saw Yvette lying on the settee. He walked over to her and saw her eyes were closed. "Come on, darling. You can't sleep down here."

But Yvette could not hear him.

"Yvette", said Richard again and got hold of her hand. "You're like ice. Come on, I'll take you back to your room." She did not respond, and after a moment Richard put his candle down on the arm of the settee and bent over her. Then he pulled her up and put his arms around her, knocking the lighted candle to the floor. In a fit of panic, he did not see it, but hugged her, and began to cry, saying her name over and over again.

He frantically looked around the room, as if he might see something that would help. But Yvette was beyond help, and in his heart he knew it. Then his gaze fell upon the portrait above the mantel. He gasped and stared in disbelief, gently letting go of Yvette's body, which lay back on the settee. There, in the portrait, was Yvette, sitting on the chair, with Thomas standing beside her. She wore a beautiful blue satin dress, her dark hair falling over one shoulder, and she was holding a single red rose. She was radiant and smiling happily. Richard froze in terror and disbelief.

Meanwhile, the candle had set fire to the carpet and one of the armchairs. It wasn't much at first, then suddenly flared up. Thick smoke began to rise. As if in a dream, Richard turned back to Yvette's body on the settee. He tried to lift it, but his strength was being sapped as he coughed, choking in the thick smoke. The flames moved across the carpet and caught the bottom of one of his pyjama legs, and dressing gown. He fell back onto the carpet, coughing. Then, a sleeve of his dressing gown began to burn. He couldn't move; he was being overcome by the smoke. He called out desperately for Maurice, but his voice was weak as he tried to put out the flames that had caught his clothing. It was no use, the fire was spreading. He fell back again, coughing and choking. He lay there, his eyes streaming, as he stared at the portrait of Thomas and Catherine.

Just then the door opened. It was Maurice. He was shocked by what he saw. He took off his dressing gown, put a handkerchief over his nose and mouth and ran over to Richard, trying to smother the flames, where they had caught his clothing. He saw Yvette on the settee, but knew he must deal with Richard first, as he was nearer the fire. With the flames on Richard's clothing out, he dragged him towards the door and into the hall, then dashed back, picked up Yvette's body, and carried it out of the room, where it lay, beside Richard, in the hallway. Maurice was exhausted and coughing violently. He thought for a moment he would collapse, but pulled himself together. He immediately closed the door of the sitting room, and opened the front door, to let in the fresh air. He felt for Yvette's pulse, but there was nothing. Then he focused on Richard. "Sir! Sir!" he shouted desperately. He patted Richard's face, but Maurice could tell by his staring, terrified eyes that he was dead. Just then a clock, somewhere in the house, struck midnight.

# Twenty-five

Peter was in bed, restless as he slept. Suddenly, his eyes opened. He lay there a few moments, not knowing where he was. Slowly, he sat up. He was untidy, his dark hair ruffled, and thick stubble on his face, making him look older than his 35 years. He was dazed, and perplexed. He looked around the room, as if seeing it for the first time. There was an oak wardrobe, large chest of drawers, a couple of small oak tables with his laptop on one, and a radiator along one wall. A fire screen covered the fireplace, and there was a chair, with his jacket and trousers over it. On his bedside table was a lamp and a digital clock, showing the time as 14.25. 29 September. The curtains were partially open, letting in a bit of light, and a gentle breeze from the slightly open window. As he continued to look around, there was a knock on the door. He turned towards it, wondering who it could be. "Come in," he said.

The door opened, and in came his butler, Michael. He was a man in his 50s, smartly dressed and carrying a silver tray on which was a silver teapot, matching milk jug, sugar bowl, and china cup and saucer. Peter watched him as he approached his bed, feeling puzzled, trying to remember.

"You're awake, sir," he said, setting the tray down on one of the small tables. "That's solved my dilemma," he continued. "I wasn't sure what to do. The doctor said you were to rest, so I didn't want to wake you."

Peter watched as Michael poured the tea. "The doctor?" asked Peter, as Michael handed it to him.

"Yes," continued Michael. "Don't you remember? You collapsed yesterday. Gave me quite a turn, I can tell you. We'd just finished taking the wrapping off the portrait, you took one look at it, then collapsed. I called the doctor immediately. You'd come round slightly by the time he arrived. But after a thorough examination, he said you were suffering from exhaustion, and to have a week's bed rest."

"I don't remember any of that," said Peter.

"I'm not surprised," said Michael. "You were really out of it. You've slept for almost 24 hours."

"24 hours?" repeated Peter, shocked.

"May I say, you're looking a lot better than you were yesterday. I was really quite worried. The sleep must have done you good." Michael walked over to the window and opened the curtains. Peter winced at the sudden brightness. Then he began putting Peter's clothes in the wardrobe. As he did so, he said, "By the way, a Mrs Patterson from the Women's Institute rang. She said she'd like you to give a talk on the 'art of becoming a successful writer'. I told her you were unwell at the moment, but you'd ring her when you're better." Michael closed the wardrobe doors and turned to Peter. "She sent you her best wishes for a speedy recovery."

Peter sipped his tea, deep in thought.

"I expect you could do with a bite to eat, sir. Can I bring you anything?"

"Actually, I'm not very hungry," replied Peter.

## THE PORTRAIT

Michael was concerned. "Perhaps just a little something, sir? It has been a long time since you last ate."

"Yes," said Peter, staring ahead thoughtfully. Then he turned to Michael. "Yes, you're right, perhaps just a sandwich, nothing more."

Michael smiled. "Of course, sir. I'll bring it to you shortly, and a fresh pot of tea."

"No, it's all right," said Peter, "I'll come down. I'd like to see this portrait."

"I think you'll be very pleased. And you were right, sir," said Michael.

"Right?" asked Peter.

"It was so damaged, half of it was obliterated, but you said you thought there was another figure underneath, where it had been smoke-damaged."

"And there was?" asked Peter.

"Yes," smiled Michael. "Catherine was revealed after the restoration work, sitting happily beside Thomas. A beautiful woman. It's amazing what restorers can do these days, isn't it?"

"Yes," agreed Peter, thinking on what Michael had just told him.

"It was always thought he'd been painted alone," continued Michael. "Now you'll be able to correct the error in the book you're writing." Suddenly, Michael noticed Peter looking perplexed. "Is anything wrong, sir?" he asked.

After a moment Peter answered. "D'you know, I've had the most incredible dream."

"Sir?" asked Michael.

Peter was deep in thought. "It doesn't matter."

"Shall I run you a bath, sir? Then I'll make your sandwich."

"No, not just now. I'll bathe and dress later. Just get my dressing gown, would you?"

"Of course, sir." As he went to the wardrobe he said, "You'll be glad to know the decoration of the main bedroom is almost complete."

Peter looked at Michael as he helped him on with his dressing gown.

"I think you'll find it more to your liking now," he continued. "You'll be able to move back within a couple of days. Will there be anything else, sir?"

"No, thank you, er..." Peter looked at Michael, embarrassed, trying to remember his name.

"Michael, sir."

"I'm so sorry, Michael," said Peter.

"That's all right, sir." He turned to leave the room, then stopped. "By the way, sir, I took the liberty of having the portrait hung in the sitting room, just as you suggested."

"Thank you," said Peter.

"But for you supervising the clearing of the attic room, it may well have been thrown out, and that would have been a great pity." He left the room.

Peter stood for a while, trying to take it all in. He looked at the clock, and saw it was now 14.45. Perhaps he should have had a bath first. He finished his tea, put the cup and saucer back on the tray, and left the room. He went into the bathroom across the corridor; looked at himself in the mirror, deep in thought. Then he decided to shave, brush his teeth and comb his hair. He went back into the bedroom, and could hear voices through the open window. He walked over and looked out. There were two young gardeners with hoes and a wheelbarrow, working to the far right of the garden. They were chatting and laughing about something.

Then they turned back to their work. Peter smiled. Then his smile faded as he focused on the garden below, quite different from his dream. There were still the paths in place, and a few rose bushes, but intermingled between them were various plants and shrubs.

After a moment he turned from the window and left the room. He stood in the corridor thinking, then walked towards what would have been Yvette's bedroom, in his dream. He slowly opened the door and saw it was being used for the storage of items from the main bedroom whilst it was being decorated. He felt surprised that he almost wished it was like in his dream. It had all seemed so real – Yvette, the Applebys, everything. He shut the door, and was just turning to walk to the staircase when he heard the sound of the door to the main bedroom at the end of the corridor, opening. He turned slowly towards it. A man, dressed in overalls, was standing there with a tin of paint and a paintbrush. He was about to paint the door jamb. He saw Peter, smiled and nodded to him.

"How do?"

"Good afternoon," replied Peter.

Just then, a younger man in overalls, carrying a step ladder across the room, looked over to him. He had on a baseball cap, turned the wrong way round. "Af'noon," he said.

Peter smiled and turned away, walking towards the staircase. The older man turned to the younger and smiled, inclining his head towards Peter, because he was still in his dressing gown, so late in the day. Then they returned to their work.

Peter walked down the staircase towards the sitting room door. Why, he wondered, did he feel anxious?

He opened the door and took a step inside. Immediately his eyes focused on the portrait, which was hanging over the fireplace, the fire burning brightly in the grate. He walked slowly over, and stared up at it. His heart almost missed a beat as he saw the beautiful woman in the painting: Catherine – his Yvette, from the dream. She was sitting on the chair, by which stood the handsome Thomas. They were smiling and looking so happy.

Now Peter realised the reason for his vivid dream. They had been unwrapping the portrait the day before, when he collapsed, Michael had said. The portrait was probably the last thing he had seen.

Peter glanced around the room. There were armchairs by the fireplace, and a settee facing it. He saw a large television set and Digibox; various tasteful furnishings, and a coffee table placed before the settee. It had a couple of magazines, some post, and a Dictaphone on it. Peter sat down on the settee and again looked at the portrait. Just then the door opened and in came Michael, wheeling a tea trolley. He took it to the side of the settee. Peter was engrossed in the portrait.

"It's come up very well, hasn't it, sir?" said Michael.

After a moment, Peter came to himself again, turned to Michael and smiled. "Yes it has, very well."

Michael began to pour the tea. Peter saw that not only had he brought sandwiches, but also cakes and pastries. "I see you've done me proud, Michael."

"Just to keep you going until dinner, sir."

Peter smiled. "Thank you."

Michael looked at the portrait. "She was a very beautiful young woman, wasn't she, sir?"

"Yes, she was."

Michael handed him his tea.

"Thank you," he said.

"Well, if there's nothing else you require, sir, I'll leave you to it."

"No, there's nothing else. Thank you, Michael."

"Very good, sir." Michael left the room.

Peter took a sip of his tea, then put it down on the coffee table. He turned to the trolley, took a small plate and napkin and picked up a sandwich. As soon as he started eating, he realised how hungry he was. Not only did he have a couple of sandwiches, but helped himself to a cake as well. He poured himself another cup of tea, then settled back on the settee. After a moment he noticed his letters, unopened, on the coffee table, along with a letter opener. He took the envelopes in his hand and looked at each one. He half expected to see them addressed to Richard Anderson. But there it was in print: Mr Peter Forbes. He smiled to himself and put the letters down. He did not want to be bothered with mail at the moment as he was still feeling tired and washed out. Then he saw the Dictaphone on the coffee table. He remembered he was writing a book on Shearwater Manor. All these things tied in with his dream, it all having been on his mind before his collapse. Curious to see how far he had got, he leaned forward and switched on the machine to play. After a few seconds his voice began to speak:

*"The history of Shearwater Manor is, indeed, a tragic one. But who could have foretold that on the 100th anniversary of Catherine's death, Richard Anderson would lose his fiancée, Yvette Moreau, and his own life, on the very eve of their wedding.*

*"The pair were found in the sitting room late that fateful night. A fire had broken out, which apparently had been caused by a candle. There had been a violent storm that night and the electricity had failed. Richard Anderson was found near the body of his beloved fiancée, as thick smoke filled the room. It was only due to the alertness of the butler, at that time Maurice Edwards that the manor stands today. He thought he had heard, although very faintly, a voice shouting in panic, and rushed to see what had happened. He was able to quell some of the flames, and get the unfortunate pair out of the room but, sadly, too late."*

Peter was listening intently, as the narration continued:

*"A postmortem discovered Miss Moreau had died of a brain tumour. But during the inquest a strange fact was revealed. Some time in her distant past, Yvette Moreau had received a hard blow to the head, which had resulted in a fractured skull. According to the pathologist, it had been a serious injury, and he was at a loss to know how she could have survived it.*

*"The events leading to the tragic death of Richard Anderson will never be quite clear. It is believed, on finding the body of his cherished fiancée, he collapsed in a state of severe shock, knocking over or dropping his candle. His death was caused by smoke inhalation and recorded as accidental.*

*"Richard and Yvette had spent their last evening with their closest friends, Barbara and Reginald Appleby, at their home, Flaxted Hall. They had noticed*

*Yvette seemed uneasy that night, and Richard had been anxious for her. They too became concerned by her manner. They had known Yvette for only a short time, a matter of weeks in fact, but had taken her to their hearts.*

*"Sadly, the Applebys also had their share of tragedy. Not long after the dreadful events at Shearwater Manor, Reginald Appleby was thrown from his horse, and was confined to a wheelchair for the rest of his days. His devoted wife, Barbara, nursed him herself for three years until his death. After which, exhausted and unable to come to terms with her loss, she entered a nursing home, and died just two months later, not from exhaustion but, it is believed, from a broken heart. A motorway now runs through where the Applebys home once stood. Flaxted Hall is no more.*

*"How would life have progressed for these four friends had fate taken a different course? Richard Anderson and his fiancée now lie side by side in the graveyard of the country church, where their marriage should have taken place. Together in death, if not in life.*

*"Although tragedy has played its part in the history of this beautiful manor, it is hoped the period of time in which the house had remained unoccupied, together with the extensive renovation it has undergone in recent years, will help lay, once and for all, the ghosts of the past, and it will be a happy and peaceful place in which to live."*

After a few moments the machine clicked off. Peter gazed at the portrait for a few moments, then got up and walked across to the window. He looked out across the gardens and parkland. He was thinking back to his dream, how real it had all seemed, and how he felt now.

A feeling of sadness came over him and tears came to his eyes as he thought of the manor's tragic past. *But it all happened a long time ago*, he thought, *and all those involved would be at peace now.*

Just then, the door opened and Michael came in. "Would you like more tea, sir?"

It was as if Peter had not heard him. Then, still looking out of the window, he asked, "Do you believe in reincarnation, Michael?"

Michael was taken aback. "Reincarnation, sir?"

"Yes," said Peter.

"Well, I haven't really thought about it, but since you ask, no, I don't think I do."

Peter turned to him and smiled. "No, neither do I."

"Do you need anything else, sir, whilst I'm here?"

"No thank you, Michael. I'll bathe and change now. I was going to shower, but I think a bath will relax me."

"Of course, sir. I'll go and run that for you now."

"Thank you, Michael."

As Michael left the room, Peter noticed his mobile phone on the coffee table and went over to it. It had several voicemail messages and texts, which would remain unanswered for a while. None of them seemed important to him at the moment. He felt weak and tired, and was going to take the doctor's advice of resting for a few days.

He left the room and made his way upstairs. The door at the end of the corridor was open. The decorators had finished their work and left. Light from the room spilled out onto the corridor, and he walked towards it. As he went into the room he felt a jolt to his system, as if expecting it to be as in his dream. But the room was bare. A carpet was to be delivered the following day, then the furniture moved back in. He walked to the front window. A gardener was raking the gravel on the drive. The window was open to help dry the paint and air out the room. The rooks were calling to each other in the trees and over the gardens. He watched the scene for a short while, then turned and left the room. He saw Michael just then coming out of the bathroom.

"Oh, sir, the bath is ready for you now."

"Thank you," smiled Peter. "I'm going to have a nice long soak."

"Very good, sir," said Michael as he walked towards the staircase.

Peter went into the bathroom, removed his dressing gown and pyjamas, and stepped slowly into the bath. The temperature of the water was just right, and he leaned back and closed his eyes. He lay there for a while, resting, and feeling all his tension drift away. After about 20 minutes, he decided to start his ablutions. The water was a bit cooler now and he reached forward to the hot tap to add some more. As he leaned forward, he noticed something on his left leg. Curious, he lifted his leg out of the water. There, as fine as gossamer, was a scar running from the outside of his foot up towards his knee. He also noticed, as his left hand gripped the tap, he had another faint scar on part of his hand and outer arm to the elbow. His heart missed a beat as he remembered, so vividly, his dream: Yvette lying on the settee; his useless efforts to bring her round; the shock when he saw the portrait, with Catherine – his Yvette – now included in the painting. He remembered coughing, as smoke swirled around him and flames licked his dressing gown, flames he couldn't put out. He had been so weak, he must have passed out with shock, and the thickening smoke. Then he felt someone putting out the flames on his clothing and pulling him away from the fire. The last thing he remembered was the portrait, as he was dragged away, the smoke swirling around it, obliterating the figure of Catherine. Then he remembered no more.

About an hour later Peter was back in the sitting room. He had poured himself a brandy and was standing in front of the portrait. Catherine's beautiful face seemed to gaze down at him, and Thomas's – such a look of happiness.

Peter held his glass up to them and said, "I know so much about you now. I think it will make a very good book. A bestseller maybe. But Catherine – my Yvette – who would ever believe me?"

# About the Author
# Dawn Woods

I wrote a few short stories as a girl and started The Portrait some time ago.

I attended university in my late forties taking Media Studies.

After an unsettled period in my life, I lived in Austria for a short while before returning to England, and eventually finishing my book.

Milton Keynes UK
Ingram Content Group UK Ltd.
UKHW012247260224
438492UK00005B/272

9 781803 817453